She didn't know whether to kiss him or kill him...

'Wow.' Awe and wonder mingled in Archer's sexy, rough voice. How could I have missed such a beautiful body? I'll keep that image of you rising out of the water, naked and shimmering, for as long as I live.'

'You'll forget it with the next nude body you see.' She sank as low as she could into the churning water. 'Which should be the day after this weekend, if you don't find some lovely thing here to play with first.'

'You've hurt my feelings,' he said. 'I'm never with more than one woman at a time.'

Her eyes widened in mock wonder. 'Is that one per hour, one per day or one per date?' she asked sweetly.

'One per bed,' he retorted with a soft laugh. 'It's a rule I have.'

Rita Clay Estrada is one of Temptation's best-loved authors. Not only has she written more than twenty books for her fans, she is also co-founder and first president of the Romance Writers of America. Before embarking on her writing career, she studied art and psychology, worked as a model, a secretary, a bookshop manager…and the list goes on to this day.

Rita is also a mother, and a woman whose family is very important to her.

ONE WILD
WEEKEND

by

Rita Clay Estrada

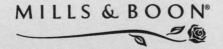

MILLS & BOON®

*All the characters in this book have no existence outside the imagination
of the author, and have no relation whatsoever to anyone bearing the
same name or names. They are not even distantly inspired by any
individual known or unknown to the author, and all the incidents are
pure invention.*

*First published in Great Britain 2000
by Harlequin Mills & Boon Limited,
Eton House, 18-24 Paradise Road, Richmond, Surrey TW9 1SR*

© Rita Clay Estrada 1999

ISBN 0 263 82375 X

21-0005

*Printed and bound in Spain
by Litografia Rosés S.A., Barcelona*

Prologue

ARCHER FELT LIKE a piece of meat in a butcher shop window on the poor side of town. Was this what a woman walking into a pub felt like when all eyes turned to her?

Although literacy was one of his pet projects and he was involved in this charity auction for that excellent cause and was getting the publicity he'd wanted in exchange for his participation, he didn't feel good about being judged. Those women out there might find him wanting, and his ego wasn't ready to deal with rejection. Blocking that thought out of his mind, he stood on the sidelines ready to walk out on the well-lit Waldorf-Astoria ballroom stage.

He peered through a gap in the curtain at fourteen hundred plus wealthy socialites who, after a sumptuous dinner were waiting to bid on each and every one of the fifty males milling around behind the curtains.

Suddenly, the lights went down, the orchestra began playing and the first of several announcers walked out to applause. *Let the games begin.*

All the bachelors lined up according to the numbers pinned to the front of their tuxedo jackets. Still in a row, they came out and took a turn around the stage so they could be seen.

This was hell, he thought. From the looks on the women's faces, he was being judged solely on his looks instead of on his own merits as a talented photographer and astute businessman. He didn't like that at all. Those who gave him no more than a cursory glance hurt his ego as much as the ones who stared and pointed. Those who were trying to judge the size of his manhood through his tuxedo pants didn't care about the fact that he was a knowledgeable lover, either. He was more than just a good lay, but they'd never know it. That wasn't the point of this auction.

Then, to a rousing applause, they—the merchandise—walked behind the curtain again. The first man to be auctioned stepped out for the bidding to begin.

Archer was number ten.

Visions of his youth slammed into him full force as he remembered the way he'd gawked at girls, not the least bit interested in who they were. He didn't know how, but he promised he'd make up for all those tasteless leers he'd been guilty of in those naive days.

He'd repent by helping others.

He'd give money to a convent.

He'd remember to think of the models he photographed as people instead of sexual marketing devices.

He'd smile at old ladies more often.

And never would he inflict this feeling of being an object on another person.

When it was Archer's turn, there was a new

announcer at the podium. With great reluctance he walked out to stroll the runway and strut his masculine stuff.

"Just look at this successful and handsome hunk, ladies. His name is Archer and he's one of the top fashion photographers in the country. He's gee-orgeous and ready for a three-day romp in one of the most luxurious resorts in the Poconos. Plus he'll give you the best he's got—a full-scale fashion shoot in his studio and around New York City!" The throaty female announcer was one of the newscasters for WONE TV in the city, and she was obviously having a ball in her role as auctioneer. "Take a good look, ladies, as Archer walks our runway in that sexy, hand-tailored tuxedo. This is one man who has more to offer than tight buns and great shoulders. He's also a wholehearted supporter of Heart Books Literacy Charity. A true romance hero who could grace anyone's covers, books or otherwise!" Titters rose in the grand ballroom. The announcer looked pleased. Archer felt worse. This was a literacy auction to raise money, not an event to support the vice squad. The woman ought to have her mouth washed out. "What more could you ask?"

Archer walked down the length of the runway just as he'd rehearsed earlier. He smiled at each woman he made eye contact with. *Romance cover hero, huh?* That wasn't bad. This was getting easier.

When Archer reached the end, he shrugged out of his jacket, hooked it on his finger and tossed it over his shoulder. Then, looking out over the audience he connected with the women, one by one. He wanted it to be clearly understood that he was more than a male body standing in front of them. He was a force to be reckoned with, and they were getting more than company for a weekend. They were getting an intelligent man who knew all about women—and how to please them.

Two women sitting at a table on the edge of the runway caught his eye. One was blond and absolutely stunning. Her blue eyes were wide and appreciative as she daringly looked him up and down. Her girlfriend, a brunette, had her eyes on Archer while she leaned toward her friend and whispered in her ear. This one had a sweet look but nothing to make him pick up a camera.

He gave the pair a sexy grin and an audacious wink. Without batting a lash, the blond and beautiful one lifted her champagne glass in silent toast. With a jaunty toss of her blond hair, she gave a slow and sexy wink in return.

He sent her a slow, sexy smile, then turned and walked back up the runway. As he stood, relaxed, by the side podium, he undid the knot in his bow tie and unbuttoned his collar.

This wasn't half as bad as he'd originally thought.

He realized he was actually having fun!

The blonde he'd winked at earlier was still staring at him thoughtfully, while her dark-haired friend talked quickly and wrote notes on a pad on her lap. Good, at least he'd have *someone* bidding for him.

The announcer was describing his talents. "...and ladies, you have the opportunity of a lifetime. Archer, the owner of Archer Photography, is gifted in more ways than one. He's in demand by the finest magazines in Europe and North America. His other talents everyone here at the Waldorf-Astoria can easily see. Rumor has it that he escorts to the "in" parties some of the most beautiful women in New York City. And we have some beautiful women, don't we, ladies? Well, I'd bet that Archer knows most of them."

The audience sighed a collective "ohhh." Archer just smiled. He didn't have a choice. He was on the block...about to be sold to the highest bidder.

"May I have the first bid, please?"

The bidding began.

Women raised their round paddles as the auctioneer continued an easygoing patter. "Come on, ladies! Don't insult the man! Look at those biceps and slim hips. He can cross any river, climb any mountain! Give him a chance to prove himself worthy of the toughest audience in the world. You."

Giggles, titters and paddles held high all blurred together. Even though this was all on the up-and-up, that meat market, cattle auction feeling was back again. Archer suddenly wished he hadn't agreed to this.

This was humbling. He'd make a statue to

Woman all over the universe. He purposely blocked out the sound of the auctioneer's voice.

"Ten thousand once! Ten thousand twice! Ten thousand final! Sold to number twelve hundred twelve! That is a Ms. Melody Chase. Congratulations, Ms. Chase."

It was over.

Archer shielded his eyes and looked at the blonde at the far end of the runway. She was grinning. Good. At least the weekend in the Poconos wouldn't be a total loss. There might even be some fun at the end of the rainbow.

"Please pay at table one at the back of the room, Ms. Chase. They'll give you the information packet." The lady from WONE breathed into the mike and almost whispered, "A little later, Archer will introduce himself to you."

The brunette nodded and rose from her seat next to the blonde.

Archer squinted against the glare of the hot stage lights. Throughout this whole ordeal, he'd assumed that anyone who bid on him wanted to be a model—that he was her ticket into that career. That's why he'd singled out the blonde. She had a chance of succeeding at flirting with the camera.

Instead, her brunette friend left the table and walked to the back of the large room. Wrong woman won the bid.

Or maybe the brunette had dreams of being a model, but he didn't see them coming true. The competition was too fierce and although she was pretty, she wasn't striking. The camera wouldn't love her.

He stepped off the stage, waving at the audience as they gave him a loud round of applause. He was proud of his performance. He was used to hiding behind the camera, not being the focus of attention. Especially not *this* way.

The next man stood in the wings looking slightly dazed as Archer passed by. "Give 'em alpha male or they'll tear you apart," he said, with a pat on the man's shoulder.

Archer chuckled at the memory of number eleven's white face as he wove through the parade of men awaiting their fate. As for *his*, he was "supposed to meet the one who bought 'em," as the Heart Books helper behind the scenes informed him in a stage whisper.

Ms. Chase, the brunette, stood by the back table, her wide, interested eyes drifting over the audience.

Giant screens in the corners captured Archer's attention. They brought the stage activities up close and personal so the bidders saw every facial expression and nuance of the present auctioned man.

"Mr. Archer?" she asked in a low voice and he brought his attention abruptly back to her.

"Ms. Chase." She was tiny—even smaller than he'd first thought. His glance darted toward the table she had occupied. The blonde was still there. He'd bet she was close to six feet.

"Melody," she replied, and his gaze flew back to her.

"Yes." She was ruffling through official-looking auction papers. "When is it convenient for you to leave?" she asked, looking up to meet his gaze.

She didn't seem to be the least bit impressed with him. He might as well get this over with. He spoke shortly. "Next weekend."

She reached into her purse, pulled out a small electronic calendar and tilted it so she could study it in the dim light. "Okay, that's fine by me, too." She looked up and the softness of her gray eyes caught him by surprise. "I'll meet you there. Okay?"

"Aren't we supposed to be traveling together?"

"Yes, but I have a workshop in Pennsylvania the day before, so I'll already be there."

He shrugged that off with a "Fine by me." He couldn't shrug off the impact of her gaze.

Melody smiled. "Wonderful. I'll see you then, Mr. Archer. Enjoy your week." She held out her hand.

Archer frowned, unwilling to accept her hand just yet. What the hell was going on here? She just paid ten thousand dollars for his company and was acting as if it were an ordinary business-as-usual kind of day.

"Wait a minute," he said. She dropped her hand, looking embarrassed. "You just paid a tidy sum for me and I don't know why. Talk to me, Melody Chase."

"Oh, I..." Her cheeks turned a rosy pink. "I didn't know we were supposed to explain here."

He took her arm firmly and escorted her to a corner where they could have a little more privacy. Letting go of her arm, he casually leaned against the wall, letting her know he wasn't going anywhere until he heard what she had to say. "This is as good a time as any, Ms. Chase. You just bid ten thousand dollars for me. And while I can see you as a philanthropist—" he glanced down and noted that while her clothes were not designer items, they were well made "—I know you didn't plunk down that money just to help people learn to read. You could have sent a check for that and never showed your face in this arena. So, what is it you expect me to do for you?"

"How do you know I didn't just need a vacation?" she countered, her gray eyes even more wide than before. She looked just a little frightened, which intrigued him.

"I'm psychic." He waited.

The tip of her pink tongue came out and dampened her lips. His stomach clenched. Then she gazed up at him as if she were facing a firing squad. "I need your expertise as a male, Mr. Archer."

"Just Archer."

"Archer," she corrected softly, "I need help." The sound of her voice was almost drowned out by applause as some other man walked down the runway.

Good grief. So he was supposed to be a knight in shining armor? He hadn't read any Heart romances, but he had a feeling the woman in front of him had. His gaze narrowed. "What kind of help?"

She took a deep breath and the words rushed from her in a whoosh. "I need some advice, really. I need you to help identify what's wrong with me so I can correct it."

He stared at her blankly. "What?"

She repeated her problem, slowly, so he was sure to soak up her words, even if they didn't make much sense to him. "I need you to tell me what's wrong with me from a male standpoint. Why men date me, then marry someone else."

He stared, this time taking in the crown of shining brown hair, the heart-shaped face, the slim body. She looked exactly like the kind of woman a guy's mother would love to have him bring to dinner. She *wasn't* the kind to drive a man into a sexual frenzy. She was too sweet for that.

He cleared his voice. "And you want to be a model."

She laughed, a soft, low laugh that echoed between them. "Not on a bet."

This wasn't adding up. Old boyfriends could tell her why she wasn't girlfriend material. She didn't need him for that. But she didn't want to break into modeling.... "Then what?"

"Then nothing. I need information about me and about the way men's minds work. And I want it from someone who isn't interested in me as a conquest. I want a totally unbiased assessment. That's all."

"And I'm not the man you want to be perfect for." It was a statement, not a question.

"I repeat, not on a bet." A sweet smile peeped out. "I promise."

He forced himself to grin to cover up his feelings. She thought she was being kind. Instead she was making him feel like a eunuch. "Well, as long as that's all you want," he said stiffly. "I'm no knight in shining armor. No Heart Books hero or anything like that."

"You haven't read any of their books, have you?"

"Nope."

"I could have guessed," she said, her tone just a trifle dry.

"But I'll be willing to if you bring one or two with you," he said, surprising both of them.

"Consider it done." She looked relieved. "I'll see you in the Poconos, Mr....Archer." She held out her hand once more.

He accepted it, feeling her softness as well as her strength. He frowned. "Just what is it you do for a living, Ms. Chase?"

She hesitated a moment before speaking. He wondered why. "I teach at New York University."

Archer whistled low between his teeth. "I didn't know university professors got paid so well."

She bristled like a bantam rooster. "I also have some money from an inheritance, Archer, not that I believe it's any of your business."

"No, of course not. I was just curious, that's all.

Ten thousand is a lot of money to give to charity in one lump sum, or to spend for a weekend."

"A chaste weekend."

He raised his eyebrows as if there were no option—mainly because there wasn't. "Of course. I understand that the press will even be there."

She looked a little flustered but still managed to maintain her composure. "Yes. I'm sure we'll be properly chaperoned."

His grin was almost wolfish, but she didn't notice. "Right. So I'll meet you there after your workshop. Have a nice week, Ms. Chase."

She flashed a smile. "Thanks."

Archer watched her walk back to the table where her friend was waiting. Her hips, encased in a long, flowing skirt swayed with every step she took in her black low-heeled boots. She was feminine and pretty in a plain sort of way. Outstanding eyes. Slim figure. And an outrageous way of treating a man whom she might be interested in snagging. And that had to be her purpose. There was no other logical explanation.

1

PARKING THE RENTAL CAR in the appointed lot, Melody glanced one more time at the directions the desk clerk at the lodge had given her. The getaway weekend with her Heart Books hero was to be spent in a secluded log cabin instead of the main lodge, and the directions were supposed to be simple to follow.

She tried to ignore the distress signals her body had been giving off since she'd finished her workshop and gotten into the car to drive here, but it was nearly impossible. Her stomach was filled with butterflies. Her knees were knocking together. And her heart was telling her it could pull the plug at any moment.

She believed all this was a message from hell, but she had no other recourse but to plunge ahead. After all, she'd plunked down ten thousand dollars to get this far. That money wasn't going down the drain just because she decided she had cold feet. She might as well plow ahead with the original plan. At this point, she had nothing to lose.

After two bad relationships, she was bound and determined to find out what it would take for her to have a man fall in love and marry her.

In her dreams, the man had a hazy face. But their baby seemed so real she could feel its tiny finger curl around hers....

So, hopefully, Archer was going to give her the necessary information to make that happen because she was ready for the next step in her life. She wanted a baby. A child. She wanted to be a mother. And with each year that passed, she wanted it more and more. With her twenty-eighth birthday not three weeks away, the biological clock was ticking loudly. She wanted to have her own family, her own someone to love. Someone besides a cat. *Tick-tock.*

The breakup of her last relationship hurt more than she was willing to admit aloud. Although she knew it had more to do with ego and pride than lost love, the loneliness ache that had been in her life for as long as she could remember was there from the time she woke up to the time she went to bed.

She wasn't a bad person. In fact, most people thought she was kind and thoughtful and nice. Although she wasn't model beautiful, she was better-than-average looking. So what was the problem?

Melody stepped out of her rental car and reached for the small suitcase in the back seat. With a flick of her wrist, she locked the car and headed down the marked and numbered path toward cabin number seventeen. Clutched securely in her other hand was the map. Twice, just for safety's sake, she read her directions.

As she checked her map for the third time, her

heel caught on a tree root and she stumbled on the path. She grabbed at the tree and muttered under her breath as her hand scraped against the bark. "Darn." It hurt.

Leaning against the tree, she soothed her stinging palm and absently looked down the path. She saw what she would have seen if she hadn't been so consumed with getting the directions right.

Her destination.

A log cabin sat nestled in the middle of a giant shard of sunbeams splintering through freshly budding trees. A light wisp of smoke curled out of the chimney and wafted through the branches above. A wraparound porch held two Adirondack chairs and a double swing, all with cushy green-and-cream-striped pads.

And Archer.

He stood at the closest corner of the porch, his arms stretched out and braced against the railing. A sunbeam sheened on his sandy blond hair and turned it almost white. The light also shadowed the front of him, emphasizing the masculine outline of his broad shoulders and lean hips.

Her throat went dry.

No wonder he was chosen as one of the fifty finest bachelors to be auctioned off for charity. He was all male and beautiful.

"Are you all right?" he called.

She must have looked like an awkward teenager! She pretended that everything was fine. Hopefully, from this far he couldn't see her flushed cheeks. "Great," she called back, trying to reach for a dignity she didn't quite have. She carefully folded the directions and slipped them into her pocket.

Archer's eyes followed her every movement as she walked the path up to the wide wooden steps. The sound of her footsteps was dulled by the blanket of leaves and needles that made up the forest floor.

As she got closer, her nerve began to leave her. She'd made a hasty decision to ask a man's advice. If it hadn't been for her best friend and the fact that it was her favorite charity, she probably wouldn't have done this at all. She wasn't sure if she was more afraid of finding out what he thought or being told she wasn't female enough, mother enough or strong enough to be a parent. Maybe he would tell her what she already suspected; that she wasn't pretty enough, sexy enough, bright enough, to keep a man. The past five years had taught her that. Now she needed to learn what to do about that. She wanted a husband and a baby—many babies perhaps.

It sounded so good....

"Hi," Archer called as he watched her approach. His gaze roved over her body, taking in and assessing each curve and plane. She felt as if she were going to get a report card any time.

"Hi, yourself," she said, giving him the same kind of appraisal. Somehow, she had a feeling that she was appreciating what she saw much more than he was. She was so plain, while everything about Archer was bigger than life. He was strong and masculine. And intimidating. She swallowed hard. There was also something deliciously out of control about him—a barely leashed sensuality.... "Have you been here long?"

"'Bout an hour." He looked around then back at her. "Different from New York City, isn't it?"

"Very. But I like it for a change, as long as I can go back." She dropped her suitcase at the front door and joined him at the railing. She took a deep breath, for the first time noticing the clean pine-scented air. "I'd miss the cab fumes and the sweet smell of garbage."

He gave a low chuckle. "And the roar of the crowd and horns on any street corner."

"And the dress-up clothes and sneaker combos on men and women."

Finally, the atmosphere was established. They had a common enemy: fresh air and wide-open spaces. It felt good.

"Have you been inside yet?" she asked, knowing she was just making small talk. She'd noticed as she walked up that smoke circled the chimney, so he had to have already been inside.

"Wait until you see the interior. It's different than anything you've ever seen in Manhattan unless you hang out in a loft in Greenwich Village with some really old hippies," he said, a mischievous grin dimpling his face.

She gave a light laugh at the image. "Sounds interesting."

"Didn't bring your friend?"

He was talking about Crystal. Men always liked her friend, and she couldn't blame them.

She liked Crystal, too. She was beautiful, witty and certainly sexy enough for ten of Melody. But Crystal didn't want to be married or have children. Ever. Ironically, she was proposed to on a regular basis and asked to be the mother of some guy's children at least once a night.

"Crystal wasn't involved in the auction."

"She didn't look like she needed to be."

That hurt. There were more beautiful women than Melody bidding on the men. Those women hadn't needed to buy handsome guys, either, she was sure. Melody remained silent, not knowing what to say next.

Luckily, he didn't think her silence was awkward. "So, Ms. Chase. Are you ready for all that you expect out of this weekend?" His voice was low and sexy and held a hint of laughter.

"I'm ready," she assured him.

"And what is it you expect?"

"Good conversation, interesting sights, new ideas exchanged, some answers to some questions."

"Wow," he said softly. "All that in the space of a weekend."

Melody chose not to go any further. Instead, she tilted her head and looked up at him curiously. "And what about you, Archer? What do you expect out of this weekend?"

He didn't hesitate. "Great photo shoot." He saw the puzzled look on her face and elaborated. "That's when photographers combine experience with light, texture and subject and get good photos. You know, like our assigned photographer is supposed to do with us as his subjects."

She nodded as if she understood. He continued. "Conversations with a woman who's not sure what she wants for herself." He shrugged. "Hell if I know. I'm just along for the charity."

"And the publicity," she snapped, unwilling to be the only one exposing herself for the weekend. "Don't forget that, Archer."

"Thank you for reminding me." His voice was dry. "But that's not why I'm here. I'm here to be of help to people who have no idea what reading is all about. To enable others to see for the first time what it's like to learn from books, to be taken away on a magic carpet ride called reading."

"To be able to spread bullstuff around as if it were fertilizer in a garden," she added.

"Now, wait just a damn minute," Archer said, his posture suddenly rigid.

Melody stared up at the stern man, unwilling to let him off the hook quite so easily. Archer stared back. Slowly—ever so slowly—the corners of his mouth tilted up in a grin. The grin turned to a chuckle. The chuckle turned into laughter. She had to join him just for the relief of it.

"Man, you know how to take the wind from a guy's sails," he finally said. "I was all ready to be totally righteous until you threw in your monkey wrench."

"Congratulations," she laughed, feeling at

ease for the first time since the auction night. "You didn't make it, either."

His brows rose, his gaze appraising her in a new light. "You wanted to be righteous, too?"

She chuckled again. "Of course. Isn't that what gets us through life? If it's not looking good and being right, what is there?"

His brown eyes narrowed, reassessing. "Damn if you're not right, again, Melody Chase."

"Stop cussing," she admonished softly. "I don't need to hear it every time you speak."

"Yes, ma'am. I'll try to remember, ma'am. But if I don't, just take it as being a part of my damn maleness."

Her gray eyes widened. "Which part? The part that doesn't think or the part that doesn't care?"

He shrugged, turning back to the scenery before them. "Either part. I don't give a damn."

"So much for being the gentleman."

"So much for wanting to know what keeps a man at your side," he said, imitating her same dry tone. "I'm beginning to understand your problem."

She grimaced, making a joke out of his words even though they'd hit home harder than she'd care to admit. "Very good, Archer. Short. To the point. Aimed directly for my ego. You would have made it, too, if I had one left."

"That bad, huh?" He was trying not to grin, and not succeeding.

"That's right." Melody stood her ground, unwilling to let Archer know just how close to her heart he had scored. After years of practice, she was an expert at hiding pain. "But others before you have taught me well, Archer. So you're going to have to do better than that if you want to get to me."

"I give up," he said engagingly, raising both hands in surrender. "Don't shoot back."

Melody turned to face him fully, hands on her hips. "Look. I don't know what your problem is, but I already told you mine. I'm not shooting back, I'm trying to get my life in order."

Archer started to open his mouth, but she pushed her pointing finger at his chest. Her gray eyes shot fire. "No, this is *my* time to talk. You can talk later. Right now, I'm telling you I don't like conflict. I don't *want* to know how you can make me cry, hurt or feel bad. I just want to know what it is about me that makes grown men leave me for some weeping baby doll who bleeds them for help and support until they propose. I want to know if it's out of the question for me to find love. Because if it is, I'll skip love and marriage entirely and head straight for motherhood. With or without a husband, I want a family."

He gave a low whistle. "Wow, lady. If you call a truce, I promise I'll do my best to compile that information and get it to you, pronto, and not make waves along the way."

She stared him in the eye. "Promise?"

"Promise."

Melody turned and looked out at the surrounding forest. She forced herself to let go of the tension stiffening her shoulders. If things got tough this weekend, she could always walk away. All she had to lose was money already spent. And it was a tax write-off. Her gaze rested on the winding path.

She hated to admit that she was scared. Crystal had talked her into this; she'd accused Melody of whining about babies, and not doing anything about it. She'd told Melody to put up or shut up. So, here she was, in the middle of a forest with a man who probably had more testosterone flowing through his veins than any five men she'd ever dated, and she was asking him for a tutorial.

She had to be insane to do this. Up close and personal, Archer was feeling even more threatening than he had up on the stage. But Crystal had insisted. What if he wanted more than she could deliver? What if she wanted to…enough!

She chastised herself for being paranoid. So what if he was all male? He had a business that he didn't want to harm, and that alone would keep him responsible for his own actions. Besides, she wasn't his type. He'd want a woman who could drive men wild. That had never been her. If it had, she wouldn't be here; she'd have already found her man. Right about now, they'd be in front of a warm fire, snuggled in each other's arms, talking about their beautiful baby who'd just gone to sleep so Mommy and Daddy could make love.

But she was here.

Melody gave a heavy sigh. Crystal was right. She might as well continue with this weekend. She had very little to lose and so much to gain.

2

"ARENT YOU EAGER to see where you're going to spend the next three days?" Archer asked, interrupting her thoughts.

Melody looked up, surprised he was still standing next to her. She'd been so engrossed… "I'm sure it's fine."

He grinned. "You could certainly call it that." He turned and picked up her suitcase, opening the front door. "I'll take this in and put it in your room."

"My room?" What was he talking about? The accommodations hadn't been discussed, but she'd assumed that the charity would work things out to everyone's satisfaction. And *her* satisfaction was to have her own place. Alone. "Are you staying here, too?"

"Of course. It's a two-bedroom cabin with a rather unusual great room in between." He looked a little sheepish. "Aw, hell. Come on in and pick your bedroom," he said, keeping the door open with his foot. "You might as well get over the shock now."

What *was* he talking about? Were the beds on the floor? Was the place a mess? She walked around him and stepped out of the bright sunlight into the dim cabin. Her eyes gradually adjusted, and it all came into focus slowly. Very slowly. She turned her head one degree at a time, taking in each and every wall, every stick of rustic, manly furniture...the hot tub.

"Hot tub?" she asked, her voice a mere whisper. "In the middle of the cabin?"

"That's what it is, all right." He sounded as if he were choking on suppressed laughter.

To the right was a small, utilitarian kitchen overlooking a large room that featured an expanse of glass artfully framing a back deck and the thick forest beyond. But it was the main room that held her attention.

Reluctantly, she stepped down into the area and forced herself to take it all in.

Two walls were paneled in a thick, rough cypress, while another wall was covered in an ornate gold-embossed material that looked as if it had come out of a seventeenth-century king's throne room. There were fat gold tassels on the matching drapes. Ornate gilded frames held copies of the Masters, the colors dark with touches of brilliant red and gold. Square in front of the rock fireplace was a "playpen couch" and behind it was a built-in black marble spa that could fit at least six bodies. Gardenia-scented steam rose from the heated water and gave the room a ghostly look.

It was the most garishly decorated room Melody had ever seen.

"Well? What do you think?"

She looked up at him, her brain unable to complete what her eyes were seeing. "Why would anyone do this to a perfectly good cabin?"

His laughter ruffled over her body like a warm bath on a chilly day. "I take it you've never been to the Poconos before?"

She shook her head, continuing to look around the room in awe. Stereo controls were built into the back of the couch, while the speakers, painted black, hung from two corners of the room. "Never."

"This is the first time you've seen anything like this?" he persisted.

"First time," she said, peeking into the deep spa. The water was crystal clear. That was a good sign, wasn't it?

"My, my, what a treat for you. The Poconos are known for honeymoon lodges and outlandishly sexy accommodations. It's a standard of tackiness every resort has to live up to." He grinned. "And you haven't even seen the bedrooms, yet." If Archer's voice could have sounded more gleeful, she didn't know how. It caught her attention.

"As bad as this?"

He nodded slowly. "You could say that. Or as good as this." He gave a shrug of his broad shoulders. "It's all about perspective."

Melody narrowed her eyes against the steam and peered at him cautiously. "What perspective? It's either in good taste or not."

Archer's face remained passive, but there was a glint in his warm brown eyes that warned her. Or was it the steam? "Not."

Her heart fell to her feet. She paid more than top bucks for three days in *this?* Her parents would have a fit if they knew—they'd wish they hadn't given her such a large share of her inheritance before she was old enough to spend it wisely.

Melody stepped away from the spa, but the damage to her hairdo was done. She felt herself losing her sleek appearance. Humidity always turned her hair into a mass of unruly curls. Thank goodness she wasn't interested in looking her best in front of this man.

She sighed. "Lead on."

Archer did. He took her arm, steering her into the bedroom to the right.

Once more, Melody's mouth opened and closed. This bedroom was also done in gold brocade. A red, padded headboard shaped like a heart topped a round, king-size bed that stopped her cold.

Melody turned to face Archer. This room looked as if it were out of a hooker's haven, and standing in the middle of it was the best-looking man she'd been this close to in longer than she could remember. She couldn't think of a thing to say, so she put on a bright smile. "What's the other one like?"

Something like admiration shone along with the laughter in his eyes for just a moment. "Right this way, young lady. I have a feeling you'll claim this beauty as your very own immediately."

It was on the opposite side of the cabin, but

with the exception of the color, it was an exact replica of the other bedroom.

"Purple," she murmured, amazed and awed that there could be so many shades of the same color.

"Purple."

"I'll take it."

Archer grinned. "I had a feeling you would."

She cast him a baleful glance. "I'm sorry. Did you want it?"

"No, no. You go ahead. This much purple is too much for me. I'll take the red and gold."

He said it with such a deadpan expression that she had to laugh. Obviously pleased at her reaction, he grinned, then he joined her in laughter. His arms came around and he gave her a light, friendly hug.

In a spontaneous response, Melody wrapped her arms around his waist and rested her head against his broad chest, hearing the sound of his laughter as it mingled with the steady thud of his heart. Her breasts tingled where they pressed against his warmth. What started as a friendly hug suddenly felt sensual.

Sexual.

Wonderful.

Archer's arms tightened. A very low, satisfied groan echoed against her ear, and he eased her closer to him. His arms tightened, inviting her to be more intimate. His strong body. His hard body. His *very* hard body!

Instantly, Melody let go, taking a backward step so quickly she almost stumbled. Embarrassed, she glanced up, and was caught by Archer's knowing look.

"The better to make love to you," he said, reading her thoughts.

"Not me." She balanced herself so she wouldn't have to lean on him again. So what if her knees were weak? She could do it. "We're not doing that."

"Nope. My head knew that. My body didn't."

"Then your head had better have a meaningful conversation with the rest of you."

He raised one eyebrow. "As long as my head knows what's going on, the rest of me does what it's told."

"Obviously not, or you wouldn't have... have..." she stammered for a word that would work. None came to mind.

"I wouldn't have been aroused?" he said with a tiny smirk.

She had to brave this out, she told herself. After all, if she hadn't made the first comment, they wouldn't be having this conversation. She looked him straight in the eye. "Yes. You wouldn't have been aroused if you were in control."

He raised that brow again. "Oh, but I would."

Her mouth formed an O and he noticed it appreciatively.

"Why?"

Archer shrugged and turned away. "Why not?" he said casually. "You're a woman and I've been celibate for a couple of months."

"A couple of months," she echoed, feeling an

irritation build to an anger. "A couple of months?" she said once more. "Good grief, you think a measly two months is a long time to be celibate?"

His answer was as simple as hers was earlier. "Yes."

"Well, now that we know each other's moral character, can we just move on to another topic?" she asked, haughtily. Good grief, she was angry because she was angry!

Archer's superior smile turned into a frown. "You don't have any knowledge of my morals, Ms. Chase. And don't brush off what I said just because you weren't the one and only cause for my arousal."

She was in way over her head. "I have not, Mr. Archer," she stated in her most stern, schoolteacher voice. "And I'd thank you to change the topic of conversation. I think your body parts have been discussed enough."

"You're right," he said, smiling suspiciously. "Let's talk about *your* body parts, instead. In case you didn't notice, you were pushing your breasts against my chest. They felt very nice, very round, but you weren't just *accidentally* that close were you?"

Anger heightened the color in Melody's cheeks. She felt as if she were about to give off steam—like the spa in the other room. She pushed back a lock of frazzled hair. "You're disgusting. I don't know why I ever let Crystal talk me into thinking you could help me!"

He gave a short bark of a laugh. "Disgusting?

Get real, Miss Chase. No woman in her right mind would pay ten thousand dollars just for a guy to give her advice. She'd go to a psychiatrist and get it for a couple of hundred." He turned and confronted her. "Isn't that right?"

Melody's anger was slowly ebbing away, being replaced by humiliation. He was right. Of course, he was right. But she had already tried other avenues—therapists and group encounters. She knew all the neat, canned answers to almost every life crisis. But she didn't have a clue as to how men thought.

That's why Crystal's idea hadn't seemed so far-fetched. Talk to an honest man who's got nothing to lose but a luxurious weekend. Of course, Crystal wasn't here.

"Right?" he demanded again.

She opened her mouth finally to admit he was right, when a knock on the front door echoed through the cabin.

A gravel-rough female voice echoed through the room. "Yoohoo! Are you two lovebirds here? It's your reporter, Shirley."

Melody snapped her mouth shut. Lucky her. She could postpone her humiliation for a while.

Archer muttered a curse under his breath. After giving Melody a dark look that promised this conversation would be continued at a later time, he walked out of the room. It was as if he'd walked into another universe, the change in him was so complete. Suddenly he was light and teasing and back to being as sexy as a cover boy.

"So glad to meet you, Shirley. I'm Archer and

my wonderful sponsor is in the other room freshening up. She'll be out in just a minute, I'm sure." Melody heard the door close. "Did you have any problem finding the cabin?"

A raspy, smoke-ridden female voice answered. "Not at all. The front desk gave such detailed directions I thought they'd never shut up, but I just took the main path, followed the signs and here I am. Duane's outside taking some shots of the cabin. How have *you* been, Archer?"

Melody should have known. One more woman who had fallen under the macho, know-it-all spell of Archer. Crystal had, and that was why Melody had bid on him. Melody had chosen number twenty-eight but Crystal had said no. She was going to kill Crystal.

Crystal had said Archer would know women better because he worked with models all day. And he'd know what men wanted because he was a man's man and the envy of other men. Besides, she'd said anyone who could make those women in lingerie catalogs look so sexy had to know a lot about the bedroom chase....

Melody heard a deeper voice with a slight Western twang entering into the conversation. The photographer. Duane. She wiped an errant tear of anger from her eye. If Archer could manage to be charming, so could she!

She walked into the room with a bright smile. "Hi, there, I'm Melody Chase," she said, extending her hand first to the reporter then to the photographer.

The reporter, who was in her late fifties and

wore tan shoes that resembled combat boots, looked at Melody oddly.

Hoping her face wasn't giving her away, Melody inquired politely about Shirley and Duane's accommodations.

"We're staying up at the lodge in much—" Shirley looked around "uh…less spectacular quarters."

Melody detected a hint of jealousy in her voice. It couldn't have been the decor, so she could only assume that Shirley was taken with Archer. Apparently, so was Duane.

He and Archer were deep in a discussion of lenses, and Duane looked as if he were hearing words from a deity.

Archer glanced over Duane's head and smiled at Melody as if they were best of friends. Melody gave a bland smile back.

Shirley scrambled in her purse and pulled out a tissue. "Here, dear. This should help that ol' mascara," she said softly, dabbing at the corner of Melody's eye.

Melody quickly took the tissue and moved to where smoked mirrors lined one paneled wall. There was a broad smear of charcoal-gray eyeliner across her cheekbone and right up to her hairline, evidence of her angry swipe.

Shirley patted her shoulder; Duane and Archer were oblivious, still talking photography. "Must be tough to be with such a woman's man, eh? Especially when you know he sees perfect women day in and day out. What made you choose him and what do you hope to get out of this week-end?"

Good grief. The interview was on.

Melody dabbed at the last smudge of the eye-liner. She needed a touch-up but she refused to do it now that Archer had seen her looking like a chimney sweep. The models he photographed were always picture-perfect. She'd be *darned* if she'd let him know her ego was wrapped up in what little looks she had. She was different than the other women in his life, she told herself, and if for no other reason, Archer would remember her because she wasn't attached to her looks.

"I know!" Shirley said, as if she'd just thought of an idea. "It's almost one o'clock, and I'm starved. How about lunch, then a walk in the woods? That way Duane can scout some loca-tions for the official photo shoot tomorrow." She looked at a tablet scribbled full of notes. "So, Melody Chase, you can start thinking about the reasons you gave so much money to literacy for Archer. And, Archer, you can come up with an answer for why you volunteered to be auctioned off." Shirley grinned. "That way, we'll all be clear on our motives, okay?"

"Fine by me," Archer said, his sexy wink visi-bly disarming the older woman.

"Sounds right to me," Melody said as she thought through excuse after excuse to bow out. "But if you don't mind, I'd like to stay here and order in. I came from a two-day conference in Philadelphia and I'm wiped out. I'm afraid I need a little downtime."

Shirley began to protest. "Oh, but—"

Archer interrupted. "You said something about a nap earlier." He looked *so* concerned. "And you do look very tired. I'll go with Duane and the lovely Shirley and stuff myself with steak and lobster, compliments of the lodge. We'll see you back here in an hour or so."

She didn't know whether to kill him or kiss him. She looked tired? The lovely Shirley? She pasted on a smile. "Thanks. I'll get rested for this afternoon."

When they left, the cabin was so silent she heard the soft wind echoing through the trees off the deck. She forced herself to relax stiff shoulders. For a little while, she wasn't on the merry-go-round. This was her time. Now.

With a lighter step she went back into the bedroom and unpacked her suitcase. She hadn't brought a swimsuit, but the spa called to her, whispering promises about her shoulders and neck relaxing under the heated water.

She checked the clock. They'd left fifteen minutes ago. If they took ninety minutes for lunch, she still had an hour and fifteen minutes. More than enough time.

She shed her clothing, twisted her hair and secured it atop her head with a giant clip. Quickly, she located a fluffy bath sheet. Still naked, she placed the towel on the side of the spa and gingerly stepped in. As her body adapted to the temperature, she eased down on the underwater bench until she was submerged up to her neck. It was heaven. She gave a luxurious sigh.

Closing her eyes, she rested her head against the back of the tub and reveled in the complete and utter peace and quiet. Once she blinked and saw the trees waving through the all-glass back wall. If she wasn't so relaxed and lazy, she would have waved back....

The front door opened with a soft click, but it could have been dynamite discharging in the silent cabin. Melody's eyes flew open and she automatically stood to flee.

She froze when she saw Archer in the doorway, a tray balanced in one hand. He looked as shocked and surprised as she felt.

"Wow." Awe and wonder mingled in his sexy, rough voice. "How could I have missed such a beautiful body?"

She sank back down under the water, blushing red-hot. "Obviously you weren't looking," she stated stiffly. "And I'd appreciate it if we kept it that way."

Archer walked toward her, not stopping until he reached the edge of the tub. Then he bent down and placed the tray next to her hand.

Melody quickly reached for controls and pushed the button labeled Jets. Instantly, water began churning, hiding her body below the bubbles. "Too late for that, Ms. Chase, ma'am. I already saw what you look like." He smiled devilishly. "And I'll keep that image of you rising out of the water, naked and shimmering for as long as I live."

"You'll forget it with the next nude body you see." She sank as low as she could into the hot water. "Which should be the day after this weekend, if you don't find some lovely thing at the lodge to play with first."

He gave a little boy pout; one she was sure had worked a thousand times before. But the look in his eyes was far from innocent. It was pure, sexy devilment. "You've hurt my feelings. I am never with more than one woman at a time."

Her eyes widened in wonder. "Is that one per hour, one per day or one per date?" she asked sweetly.

"One per bed," he retorted with a soft laugh. "It's a rule I have. Keeps me on the straight and narrow." He was baiting her and they both knew it. But there was something titillating about the way he said it. If anyone else had dared to be this outrageous with her she would have been shocked. But Archer was different....

"You're disgusting," she said with no conviction in her voice.

"And you're prim and proper on the outside. But I'd bet you're a bundle of sexually repressed nerves on the inside. You and I both know it. The only difference between us is that I admit what I am, and you hide what you are."

"Are you to be complimented for showing your failings, Archer? Or excused?" Her gray eyes weren't soft right now. They spoke of determination to put him in his place.

He smiled, a sexy, wolfish smile. "Envied," he said softly. "And admired."

Suddenly the bubbles weren't enough cover. She crossed her arms over her breasts, knowing she couldn't play this game against such an experienced player. It was time to call it off. "Please leave."

"Not yet."

"Please."

Archer sighed. He ran a hand through his blond hair and it fell right back into place. "Okay, I'll let you off the hook this time. I just brought you a sandwich and fresh fruit with a glass of iced tea. I had a hunch you wouldn't order anything to eat and I didn't want you fainting on us this afternoon."

As if to emphasize his last words, her stomach growled. At least he couldn't hear it over the sound of the bubbles!

She'd forgotten the tray he'd come in with. She was both surprised and touched and felt just a little guilty. After all, she had baited him first. "Why, that's so nice. Thank you. I appreciate it."

"Nothing to it," Archer said as he stood. She followed him up with her eyes, noticing once more how long his legs were and how well he filled out a pair of jeans.

She quickly looked back at the tray. "Thank you for your thoughtfulness."

"I bet," he said softly, "you send thank you notes, and bring hostess gifts, always say 'please' and 'thank you' and never say a mean word. And, never, ever, color outside the lines."

In spite of his gentle tone she felt attacked again. How could he make her feel defensive about thanking him for his generosity? "There's nothing wrong with that."

"No, but there's nothing wrong with coloring outside the lines, either. Sometimes it makes a whole new picture. You ought to try it, just to see the difference."

Obviously, he was enjoying baiting her. She wouldn't allow her agitation to show. Instead, she'd state the obvious and let it go. "I have an imagination, Archer. I don't need to do something in order to know how it would feel or look."

His brows rose in disbelief. "Really? I'd like to probe that thought a little deeper, Ms. Chase. But right now, my own lunch is waiting." He turned toward the door, casting a parting shot over her shoulder. "And you're turning into a prune."

Before she could think of a retort, he was out the door.

Lost in thought, Melody turned off the bubbles, stepped from the spa and wrapped herself in the bath sheet. She was weak from having spent so much time in the tub. Her knees were wobbly, her ankles barely held her in an upright position. Carefully picking up the tray, she walked with measured steps into her purple bedroom, steadying herself as she reached the large, round bed.

Making herself comfortable was easy. She propped all the pillows behind her and stretched out, placing the tray on her lap. Instead of reaching for the book she'd put by the side of the bed earlier, she stared at a painting of a forest that hung on the far side of the wall. But her thoughts were elsewhere.

Archer.

Everything about him reminded her of barely leashed sexual energy—the way the sun glinting on his blond hair made him look like a lion, the way he walked across the room, the way he was with a woman...any woman. It all added up to a man who was certain of his sexual prowess. That sensuality was the first thing that had caught Crystal's eye—and it was the first thing that Melody decided was a strike against him.

But Crystal hadn't listened.

"Melody, pick someone like him and have a little fun," she'd said.

"He's too cocky," Melody had whispered. "I want someone I can get along with a little better, someone not so..."

"Sexy? Masculine?" Crystal had answered back, her tone acid. "For heaven's sake, Melody. This isn't the time to play it safe! You want an honest opinion from a man who attracts women like a magnet. So go to the man of all men. He looks like he fills the bill to me!"

Crystal was as definite as Melody was unsure, and Melody had to rely on her judgment, she knew men so well. There was never a night she didn't have a date, if she wanted one. But Crystal had made up her mind years ago that she'd never marry. Men change after marriage, she'd said often enough, though. Melody didn't have a clue—every one of her long-term relationships had wound up leaving her and almost immediately proposing to someone else.

Jerry, the latest one, had only broken up with

her five weeks before a mutual friend told her that he and his new girlfriend had flown to Las Vegas for their wedding, and, no, it wasn't a shotgun wedding.

That news had hurt. Boy, it hurt! Most of the hurt was centered around her ego, but that didn't help make it any less painful. Two weeks after Jerry's wedding, Crystal had pitched the bachelor auction and Melody hadn't taken much convincing. As crazy as Crystal's plan was, it simmered in the back of Melody's brain like an all-day pot of spaghetti sauce—tasting better with each passing hour. Why not get someone, anyone, to tell her what it was that made grown men run in the other direction only to marry the next woman in line?

Was she dumb?

Was she asexual?

Was she ugly?

What?

If she didn't like what he had to say, all she had to do was ignore his advice. But she knew, now, that Archer *did* have the answer.

Archer. Sophisticated, sexy, intelligent, social-climbing Archer had the answer.

"Darn," she whispered, picking up a slice of tomato that dropped to her wraparound towel and placing it back on her plate.

3

Archer stared down at Melody, curled on her side on the bed. The towel was still wrapped around her slim body—barely. One hip was exposed and one long leg was splayed across the comforter.

Her chestnut-brown hair was tousled and framing her face with damp little curls, sweet as a baby's against her creamy skin. His fingers itched to touch.

Her skin was clean of the morning's makeup and flawless, her profile was perfect. She was beautiful, in a warm, natural way.

For the past fifteen years, Archer had been around women almost twenty-four hours a day. He wasn't immune to a beautiful face. But they were just faces passing through his life.

But this damn woman was different. It was going to be a hell of a weekend.

When she stood up from the hot tub in alarm, her body wet and sleek—well, *damn*. His reaction was instantaneous! He wanted her. Right there in the hot water, he wanted her in the worst way.

He'd told himself, too bad she wasn't a little more lax on the morals, or a little less uptight. She really wasn't his type. Yet he drooled over her, anyway. So, of course, he'd insulted her with every sexual innuendo he could muster. And still she kept her dignity.

Her lashes fluttered. She stretched her arms, then stopped. Very slowly, she turned her head and those large, sleepy gray eyes stared up at him. For just a moment, he saw the slumbering sensuality hidden just below the surface and his body reacted instantly. Then he saw in her face that his presence had registered. The walls came down, shutting away that vulnerable part of her that he'd seen shining from her fathomless eyes.

"Hi," he said softly, regret lining his tone. He wished he hadn't given her such a hard time; now she'd never let him inside her thoughts....

"Hi," she said, tugging the towel closed over her hip, obviously afraid to move in case some other body part was disclosed.

"I came back a few minutes ahead of the others. I wanted to apologize for my behavior earlier," he said softly, hoping he looked appropriately sorry for his sins.

He must have succeeded because she smiled so sweetly it touched his heart as well as other body parts. "Thank you for that," she said, her voice still husky from sleep.

Archer sat on the edge of the bed, his arm pinning her next to his body. "How are you feeling?"

She thought for a minute, as if taking inventory. "Rested," she said, almost surprised. "Wonderful."

Reaching out, Archer brushed her cheek with

his knuckles. She was as soft as she looked. His fingers drifted down her cheek to her neck before stopping. "You do feel wonderful, but how are you doing?"

She gave a soft laugh and the sound was heaven to his ears. He stared down at her mouth, watching it move. It was a fabulous mouth that brought all kinds of images to mind. He wanted to act on those images. Instead of reasoning it out, he did what his body told him to do.

He covered her mouth with his own and felt the silkiness of her lips as they molded to his. She was soft and sweet-smelling and so very, very gentle with him. Her hands came up to touch his chest—whether to push him away or bring him closer, he wasn't sure because they just rested against him.

He tasted her lips and tested her tongue, his own darting in to foray. He felt her breath catch in her throat, and he waited patiently. Slowly, ever so slowly, he felt her own timid response. Her tongue darted out to touch his. Then she grew more brave and felt the outline of his lips, testing, seeking, becoming more brazen. Her hands drifted up his chest, felt his muscled shoulders and circled his neck, where her fingers enjoyed the springiness of his hair at his nape.

His stomach clenched in reaction to the messages her heated mouth was sending. But he was in charge. Or he thought he was. A low moan rose from his chest, and, as if in sympathy, Melody clasped his neck and drew him even closer to heaven. Her breath was light, as if she couldn't catch enough air—or enough of him. Their tongues touched, soothed, gently dueled. And Archer realized just how susceptible he was to this little, nondramatic female.

Looking at her looking at him, he had to reverse that thought. She was dramatic all right. The soft longing in her eyes confirmed it.

He wasn't sure if he was ending the kiss to spare her—or to spare himself. He pulled away reluctantly, nuzzling her neck and the soft underside of her chin, ending up at the base of her throat where the pale skin pulsed with her heartbeat. Her pulse was beating so fast, telling him exactly what her reaction to his kiss was. She was just as excited as he was.

Normally, he would have no problem taking this woman, right on the bed, right now. For some reason, even though his body was more than ready, he didn't want to make love to Melody yet.

Not yet.

Not yet! He clenched the bedspread into a knot. Not yet…

Melody sighed, her hands coming from behind his head to push gently against his chest. He had expected that action when they first began, but he was surprised that she did it now.

He wasn't ready to let go. His mouth brushed and kissed the very top of her breasts, her magical softness begging him to explore further.

"Archer, don't," she murmured, her voice as breathless as he felt. "Someone's coming."

The knock on the door stopped whatever

words he was about to stay. Instead, he hollered. "Just a minute!" But when he got to the bedroom door and reached to close it, he looked back and was caught by her expressive gray eyes. Her wanton pose, bare skin, and the taste of her still on his mouth made him growl with thoughts he didn't know he had. "Damn," he said in a low, rough voice.

Melody's lashes touched her cheeks slowly then opened again to pin him to the spot momentarily. "Don't curse," she said.

The knock intruded on the room again. Archer shut the bedroom door hard, stomped to the front door and opened it with a glare.

Shirley and Duane stood there, a little shocked at his look and he tried to wipe away the irritation he felt at their intrusion. "Sorry, I was out on the deck, uh, meditating. Didn't hear you right away," he lied.

"Oh," Shirley said, clearly surprised. "Do you do transcendental or visual?"

Archer didn't know the difference, so he picked one. "Visual."

"How wonderful! So do I!" she said. "Do you ever do transcendental?"

"On occasion," he said casually, but he wasn't willing to take it any further than that. He gave his best sexy smile. "Melody is sleeping. I don't know when she'll be up. Can we meet you in the lobby in an hour or so? That will give me time to unpack, too."

Duane looked irritated and bored. Shirley looked disappointed. "Oh, I see. Well…"

"We'll be sure to give our best after we unwind a little. After all, today was a traveling day," he said.

"Of course." Shirley took a few steps backward. "Why don't you just give us a call when you're ready?"

"That's just great. Thanks." Without another word, he closed the door and turned toward Melody's room.

He knocked. "Melody?"

"I'll be out in a minute!" she called, and he knew the moment was lost.

"Damn," he muttered under his breath. If they hadn't knocked...if he had moved a little more swiftly, if he'd...

He stopped a moment and listened to the voice inside his head.

What was he thinking? She wasn't a conquest! He didn't get points for marching her to bed, for glory's sake! Besides, this wasn't the kind of woman he usually tumbled for, and he didn't need to start now! This woman had wedding bells hanging around her neck and was looking for a matching pair around some other poor guy's neck, for God's sake!

He had to get his head together.

He did what he said he'd been doing earlier. Archer walked out the sliding glass doors to the deck. Leaning against the railing, he stared through the trees to the carpet of fern. And he meditated on his life.

It had taken him fifteen years to get to this rung in his career. It had been a long hard struggle from the run-down hole of a trailer park in Atlantic City where he grew up, to the studio and apartment on the East side of New York City.

It had begun with a Boardwalk photographer who had taken him under his wing when Archer was a streetwise eleven-year-old. Under the guidance of the old man, he worked hard at the craft. He set up the camera, took many photos of people walking the Boardwalk, and sold them the goods with a winsome smile, an audacious wink and compliments that rolled off his tongue in lies sweet enough for old ladies to buy. With pride, he collected the money and turned it over to Mr. Lemon as if he were entrusted with the world's savings. And old Mr. Lemon would smile, then give him another tidbit of photographic advice to chew on.

By the time Archer was seventeen, he was running the business. But his passion was photographing the sensual, romantic figures who hung around the Boardwalk. Women who walked with style and grace and naiveté, old ladies with long-sleeved dresses and broad-brimmed hats, young girls parading from store to store in pastel sundresses and bright lipstick. He could photograph any woman and capture a part of their personality and beauty that they might never have seen before. He knew the camera so well he could make love to a woman through the lens.

When Archer was nineteen, Mr. Lemon died of a heart attack. He was sitting on the very Boardwalk bench he'd sat on for over thirty years. When all the hoopla was over and he was buried, Archer took the cameras and left, hitching a ride to the capital of fashion photography.

When he landed in New York, he lived in the garage of a carriage house in Brooklyn Heights. It sounded glamorous, and it was anything but. He had a space heater, a beat-up couch and a half bath—the bare necessities. It was a place, though, and he went to work for another photographer who didn't know half as much as he did. In the process of teaching his boss, he clarified his own techniques.

Two years later, the company landed the contract for a small mail-order catalog company in upstate New York. Archer caught on fast, realizing he could sell himself, his talent and his commitment to a good product. He made the rounds of every mail-order house on the Island and in New England, honing sales skills that would carry him for years to come. Six months later, they had several contracts. A year later, they were rolling in dough.

That was when he dropped his first name and began using his last name only, creating a logo using the name curled around the bottom of a longbow. A logo. It worked. In eight years, Archer's name had come to stand for excellent fashion photography, delivered on time, professionally managed.

In a world of temperamental artists, lack of commitment, lateness, fluctuating overhead and nondelivery, Archer was unique. He was an enigma the magazine industry wanted. He made every deadline on time. He insured space for the models to get ready instead of cramping them into a bathroom already seconding as a photo lab. They loved the large mirrors he set up as well as the privacy and space to dress without being ogled. But most of all, they seemed to like his professionalism; he never called them names or spoke down to them.

Archer was renowned as being gifted, a little flamboyant, but always professional.

When Archer's partner dropped out of the company he took a good chunk of the money they'd earned, but that was fine with Archer. He cut the huge, empty space of the studio in half, moved into a corner of the studio behind drop cloths and worked harder than he'd ever worked before, not spending a dime on himself. Instead, he updated and bought equipment.

His lenses were ground in Switzerland and Germany, his cameras were the best money could buy. His lighting and lab supplies were the newest and most innovative in the business. And it paid off. The auction was proof that he'd made it in the world of movers and shakers. Heart Books had only accepted fifty bachelors and the emphasis was on those up-and-coming, ambitious and socially acceptable men for whom prominent women would pay the price demanded.

Archer was one of the first to be asked. Not bad for a kid from Atlantic City who lived by wits and talent instead of training and education. Not bad at all...

He heard Melody's steps just seconds before he smelled the scent of her perfume. She came and stood beside him, her gaze drawn to the same group of trees he'd been absently staring at.

She breathed deeply of the pine scent and said, "I didn't realize the cabin backed up to a ravine." Her voice was low and husky, as if she were imparting sensual information. She looked over the edge of the railing. "Beautiful, isn't it?"

Although Archer didn't usually photograph scenery, his fingers itched for his camera. "Wonderful. Relaxing."

Melody laughed, but he could tell she was still embarrassed about their earlier encounter. "You sound relaxed," she stated dryly.

He gave a rueful grin and tried to release the tension in his shoulders by moving them in circles. "Sorry. Guess I got a little uptight. You weren't at lunch having to be nice to two people who were relentless in pursuing their own agenda."

"What does that mean?"

"It means that Shirley wants to tell our story her way, whether it's true or not. Duane wants to take pretty pictures of trees without people messing up the landscape. And I need the publicity for my own company, so I'm wanting them to keep us in their focus."

"Oh," she said. There went that wonderful word again, forming her mouth into a delicate circle. She looked so damn cute doing it, and he wished he hadn't seen it again. He was certain she didn't have a clue how very sensuous she looked.

Imagine that.

Archer stared over the side of the deck and caught sight of the whispering brook below. Shifting to stand behind Melody, he took hold of her shoulders and brought her in front of him, still facing the trees. "If you crane your neck a certain way and hunker down just a bit, I bet you'd be able to see around that flaming maple and spot the brook."

Melody did as she was told, loving the feeling of his thumbs stroking her neck. Following his directions, she craned her neck exactly right. "I can see it!"

"Now," he said, his voice soft and sexy in her ear. "Stay that way until you've had enough. Then turn and wrap your arms around my body and ravish me."

Melody froze. Then, very slowly she looked over her shoulder at him. Her expression said it all.

He grinned. "I had to try. Who knows? You *might* have gone for it."

Her laughter made him feel better about his teasing. Her smile was a delight, doing his soul a whole lot of good—to say nothing about his body's reaction.

"I'll make a deal with you," Melody said. "We'll do the shoot and I promise to behave myself if you promise to behave yourself."

"And if I don't?"

"Then I won't, either."

"And what's your idea of misbehaving?"

She didn't have to think for a moment. "I'll make a face in every photo, so none of them can be used for publicity."

"You'd do that?" Archer asked, pretending to be stunned at the dastardly deed. "It would ruin the charity's publicity efforts."

Melody laughed again. "Yours and theirs. Not mine. I already paid ten thousand. I don't need the publicity."

"Ohh, you're cold, Melody Chase. Very cold."

"That's right," she said in a singsong voice. "So you'd better behave or I'll get this ugly mug going and you'll lose everything you walked the plank, uh, runway for."

"Gotcha," he said, as if resigned to his fate. "I'll be nice and kind and mannerly. I'll even pull out your chair and guide you through the forest by taking your arm."

Melody pretended satisfaction. "That's more like it," she said. "So behave."

"Lady, I am," he said, knowing that he had just been tested on willpower. He wanted to hold her. He wanted to taste her mouth again. The palm of his hand itched to touch her breast. Damn! He was like a teenager obsessed with the new girl in class. "I'm making it look a whole lot easier than it is."

She kissed his cheek. "Thank you for the compliment. A woman likes to feel wanted, even if it's only a token show."

He wasn't about to admit that it wasn't his line

of bull. He was feeling vulnerable enough as it was. Hell, he couldn't even look at the woman without remembering how sleek and sexy she looked when she rose out of the steamy spa. Hell, in his job he'd seen a million half-naked women. But this one... He stopped thinking and went on automatic pilot. "You're welcome."

She gave one more look at the trees and reluctantly turned toward the door, ready to begin the photo session.

"Tell me something, Melody Chase."

"Anything as long as it means delaying the interview with those people."

He didn't smile. "What's the real reason you're here?" he asked. "Like you said, the money came from an inheritance, and you don't need the promotional stuff. So why?"

"I told you. I'm looking for some answers. You may be able to supply them."

"On how to get a husband," he repeated.

She shook her head. "Oh, no. You misunderstand. I don't need a husband. What I wanted was someone to love, but that hasn't happened yet. If you can help me figure it out, that's great. But if you can't, I'm having a baby before I'm thirty anyway."

"And grow your own someone to love?"

Her eyes met his. "Exactly."

"Don't you think that's selfish?"

"Why? Women have raised children alone for years." She shrugged. "The system has worked so far."

"No, it hasn't," he answered, disgust lacing

his voice. "Take it from someone who was raised with only a mom. It's not a pretty picture. The workload is tough and life is lonely and economically hard."

Her gaze softened. He knew she was reading between the lines. "Sometimes being raised with both parents isn't much different, Archer. Money doesn't have all that much to do with loneliness."

"Rather be lonely-rich than lonely-poor, but I'd rather not be lonely at all. Is that it?"

"That's it."

"Sounds…lonely, no matter how you put it."

"It is." Her voice was hard and he knew that whatever her experiences, they came from the heart. "Are you ready?" she asked, but her wide gray eyes searched his as if trying to find something.

He returned her gaze in the most unemotional way he could, then stared back out at the trees. "Let's go, then. But say goodbye to peace for the rest of the afternoon, missy. Shirley and Duane won't let up for a minute. Take it from someone who ate lunch with them."

With determination to get through this weekend with the least amount of hassle and the most amount of publicity, Archer took Melody's hand and led her out of the cabin, locking it securely behind them.

MELODY WAS HAVING a wonderful time. Duane was witty and his dry sense of humor was direct and to the point. Shirley, for all the stars in her eyes where Archer was concerned, was one heck of a good reporter. Her questions were right on target and her memory was wonderful.

The four went up the side of the hill in the only working ski-lift basket and stood on the stone patio of a closed restaurant. The view was stupendous, the company wonderful and Archer was more relaxed and funny than she'd known he could ever be. Not that she knew him so well, she reminded herself. In fact, she didn't know him at all aside from his reputation for business and his way with women.

Everywhere they went, Archer held her hand, helped her on and off the lifts and walked in front of her down the rock-strewn paths. They moved from one photographic moment to another. At each site, Duane got them into a wonderful pose with the richness of a forest background and the deep-blue sky over their heads.

Shirley, on some kind of inner schedule, directed Melody and Archer to the chasm bridge outlook. The fiery, late afternoon sun was beginning the evening show by sinking over the edge of the mountain, setting the forest ablaze with color.

Melody felt as if she were acting in a school play, as if she could be anyone she'd ever wanted to be. This charade with Archer was okay for the moment. It was liberating to become a Melody she didn't know, with these few people who were seeing her for the first time.

Archer spanned his hands around Melody's waist and acted as if she weighed no more than a feather as he lifted her atop the stone fence over-looking the chasm below. She rested her hands on his shoulders, keeping them there after she was comfortable. It was fine because his hands didn't leave her waist, either.

"Are you okay?" he asked, solicitously.

"I'm fine. But you'll have to hold on to me for as long as I'm here, or I might fall off...." She batted her lashes at Archer in teasing exaggeration. She felt like another person, one far more free and easy and not quite so uptight and straitlaced.

His hands soothed her hips. "In that case, we'll have to stay like this until Duane tells us other-wise." He nuzzled her neck. "And I have you ex-actly where I want you."

She bent her head to the side to give him better access. "Not really, because if I yell I'd have plenty of help getting away from you."

"Are you gonna yell?" he asked, nibbling on the outer shell of her ear.

"Yes." She gave him way to the underneath of her chin.

"Damn," he muttered. "I should muffle you before you scream."

"Too late," she whispered softly. "Help. Help. Oh, dear me, help."

"Your screams won't help. I'm going to ravish your lithe young body until you have no strength left to fight."

"So you say," she said in his ear.

"Or to move out of my arms."

"Or to get away."

"You're mine to hold so close you can barely breathe."

"And to make me feel all the muscles in your back, one by one." Her voice was so soft he had to bring his ear right to her mouth. She flicked her tongue around the rim before touching him with her heated breath.

Being in the Poconos with a sexy symbol of a man was what fantasies were made of. Here, out of her element, she could be anything and do anything. It was a sensuous side of herself she'd never explored. And wonder of wonders, it really worked! Archer thought she was sexy!

He groaned.

His mouth brushed the top of her breast through the thin T-shirt she'd worn. He did it again. And again.

Her heart beat so quickly she thought it would fly out of her chest. She wanted Archer. She'd never felt so reckless and she didn't care. She felt as blazing as the sunset. She wanted him so much that she was willing to forget that they were in the middle of a park with newlyweds on every trail, behind every tree and in every hot tub.

"Okay, Archer and Melody!" Shirley's voice sounded loud in the quiet. "Look over here at Duane. Here!"

Melody felt her face flush. Even as a teenager she'd never been caught necking out in the open, especially not with a photographer documenting her crimes. She was out of her element and it felt slightly dangerous, and exciting. She wondered briefly if she should be ashamed of her behavior, but with the warm, intimate look in Archer's deep brown eyes, her worries slipped away on the soft spring breeze.

"Dinner tonight is just for the two of us," Archer stated. He wasn't asking for permission to exclude the others.

Melody nodded because she couldn't find her voice.

"Smile!" Shirley called, standing next to Duane from the very edge of the ravine.

They both did as they were told.

Archer's warm hand remained resting firmly at her hip, reminding her that after this photo session she would be alone with him.

THE PHOTO SESSION ended at twilight. Archer strolled toward the lodge with Duane while Melody listened halfheartedly to Shirley talk about her freelance career and all the places she'd been and the interviews she'd written. It was interesting, but the real focus of Melody's attention was on the conversation behind her. Although the two men were discussing camera preferences and exchanging tips, it was obvious that Archer was the one in charge. Duane hung on every word.

They had beers in the lodge bar and shared stories and popcorn until the sun had entered another part of the world.

"Well, this has been a great time," Shirley announced with satisfaction as she reached for the last bit of popcorn. "When do you want to meet for dinner?"

"Tomorrow night around seven," Archer said before Melody or Duane could speak up.

"Oh, but…" Shirley began.

"But we all need an enjoyable evening alone to catch up from travel and fun." Archer raised his hand to get the attention of the waitress and scribbled in the air so she knew he needed the check. His smile insured fast service. "Let's face it, folks. We're all ready for a little downtime. And as long as our man Duane gets the shots he wants at dinner tomorrow night, there's no harm done, is there?"

"Well, yes," Shirley said, a frown forming. "But we're better off doing it tonight, and that way if there's anything wrong we can make it up tomorrow night."

"Shirley, Shirley," Archer said, shaking his head. "There won't be anything going wrong. Duane knows what he's doing. Have a little faith in your partner."

"Yes, but—"

Archer stopped her by standing and holding out his hand to Melody. With a great deal of relief, she accepted it and stood, too. "We'll meet you tomorrow for breakfast. Around ten?" he asked, changing the subject. "We'll be ready for whatever you have in mind tomorrow, Shirley." His gaze shifted to Duane. "And by the way, there's a delightful little brunette who checked in just a few minutes ago. I didn't see a ring on her finger, either."

Duane glanced toward the lobby, grinning. "I'll have to check that out," he said. "I'm glad I've got a free evening to relax."

"See you both later," Archer said. From him, it sounded like an intimate promise.

"Bye," Melody said with a wave of her hand. She'd never allowed herself to be led out of a room by a big, strong man before, and was always irritated by those who were. But, for the first time in her life, she understood the feelings involved. It felt good to allow the man to lead once in a while—especially knowing she could change that lead with the blink of an eye.

"Nice," she said aloud, surprising both of them.

"What is?" he asked as they walked out the back door of the lodge, through the garden, over the bridge and into the carefully forested path that led to their cabin.

"Letting you lead for a while." She couldn't be accused of lying.

Archer stopped in his tracks. "Lead? As in leading you down this merry path to sin?"

"Yes," she said, laughing. He didn't realize just how little sin she'd ever been involved in. Heck, she hardly knew what sin was, how could she possibly lead the charge toward sin? "I haven't followed anyone or anything very often. But right now it feels good."

Archer shook his head. "Well, well, well, Melody Chase. I think we might have found a lesson for you to learn."

"What are you talking about?"

"Didn't you say you wanted to know what made men stick around?"

That wasn't quite what she had said, but the thought was intriguing. "Well..."

"Then, allow me to continue leading you this evening and let's see what happens."

"Well..."

"Deal or not?" he said, his handsome face less than a foot away. She forced herself not to kiss his chin.

"Deal," she sighed.

"Good." His voice was laced with satisfaction and he turned, continuing down the path toward their cabin. "Now, my lady, we're in for a night of learning."

"Good grief, what have I gotten myself into?"

Archer ignored that question. Instead, he hustled her down the trail.

Melody Chase knew she was about to learn far more than she'd dreamed. She was excited, but not afraid. She told herself that it was because she knew she was her own woman and not some mindless little female who didn't know what to do on her own. She could take back the lead at any time.

Maybe.

4

As soon as they reached the covered porch of their cabin, Archer grabbed Melody under her knees and swung her up and into his arms.

"Archer!" she cried out in surprise.

He acknowledged her shout with a wide grin and strode across the threshold of the cabin. She held on, arms locked around his neck, feeling the sheer power of happiness well up inside her, filling her until she had to laugh aloud with the pure joy of it.

"Now this isn't just done for weddings and injuries, sweetling," Archer stated. "Just for the hell of it, we're gonna do something different. Break that mold, Melody. It's time to sing a different tune. Sex for the fun of it is more exciting than sex for babies."

"Just because you want sex doesn't mean I do."

He gave a grin that made a lie out of her words. "Like hell you say."

But she stuck to her guns. "I'm looking for a commitment. A baby."

"So practice on me, as long as you realize it's only practice and never for real."

Entering the darkness, he stood still for just a

moment. Darkness surrounded them. They stood in the intimacy of silence and became still while their eyes adjusted. Melody still clung to his neck, worried that at any moment he'd drop her. After all, in her misery, she'd gained three pounds in the past month. Damn those chocolate-covered coffee beans! But what the heck, a girl had to have *something* to do with her hands!

All thoughts of weight problems fled as Archer let go of her legs and slowly lowered her to the floor. His dark-eyed gaze was as heated as the sunset had been, melting her insides.

"Talk to me, Melody Chase," he said, as a slow sexy smile began in his eyes and worked its way to his mouth. "Tell me what lessons you need to learn and let's work on them. Together. I can help even if I'm not the one for the long haul."

She stared at him, her arms still around his neck. "Lessons?"

"Yes. Isn't that what you just spent a fortune to learn? About men in general?"

"Of course, but..." How could she say this wasn't the time? That she wanted to be held and cuddled and told how wonderful she was and made to feel as if she were as light as a feather when she knew she wasn't?

Suddenly she felt awkward. This was too intimate a setting and she wasn't prepared for it. And Archer wasn't the right man. Not the right man at all. Old patterns raced to the forefront and she cast her gaze around the room, seeking a place to hide—a place to go where her emotions could air out without him seeing her turmoil.

"I know what," he said, as if he'd just thought of whatever he was going to say, when she knew darn well he hadn't. Whatever it was, he'd thought of it a very long time ago. "Why don't we order dinner, get into something comfortable and relax. After dinner, we'll talk the evening away."

"Wonderful," she said, relief in her voice. A reprieve.

Mentally, she flicked through the inventory of everything she brought with her. There was nothing sexy or sweet about her clothing. Her pajamas were plaid flannel.

He kissed the tip of her nose and turned toward his own room. "I'll meet you back here in a few minutes. Find the menu, will you? It should be in one of the kitchen drawers."

Melody did as he asked, finally spotting it in the living area. She made a note of what she wanted and left the open menu on the bar. "It's on the bar and so is my choice. Call it in when you get a chance, okay? I'm taking a shower."

"Want company?" Archer called.

"No, thank you," she said, prim and proper. "I can get the job done by myself."

She walked into her bedroom and the door closed behind her with a decisive click.

ARCHER CURSED himself for his big mouth. His imagination had got him in trouble again. He'd thought of Melody slipping into something sexy for his delight and pleasure, and never got beyond that point. All he brought with him was a pair of black warm-up pants and a gray V-neck sweatshirt. Suave and sophisticated, it wasn't.

Practically stomping into the kitchen, he glanced at the menu, picked up the phone and ordered. They promised delivery within a half hour.

He grabbed some wood from the pile on the deck and built a fire in the rock fireplace. It took time to catch, but when it finally did it took the chill off the night air that permeated the room. Besides, it was more romantic eating in front of a fire than a TV.

The sound of running water in the pipes told him that Melody was probably nude and getting ready to step into a large, purple shower. She'd probably lather her body with the liquid soap in the dispenser and rub her skin all over until it was wet and slick....

God, he was insane to torture himself this way! What the hell was the matter with him? He could go to any nightclub and find all the beautiful women he wanted. Hell, he could stay in his studio and do the same thing. He could have his pick! The problem was, he didn't want his pick or he would have already made it.

Melody just reminded him of home and family, that's all. She reminded him of those old-fashioned values he'd heard of in other families growing up. Melody reminded him of those moral values that were so rare in his jet-set world, that's all. It wasn't as if he actually wanted that kind of home and family.

Right now, with Melody, it was like playing

house. As long as he was willing and she was willing, there was nothing wrong. Hell, in a few days they'd each go their own way and this would be a cool memory to hang on to but not take too seriously. She was looking for a commitment and he was looking for…for nothing but leading his own life his own way. No encumbrances. No marriage and moonlight for him. No diapers and baby talk could take the place of a good restaurant, a maître d' who knew you and a woman on your arm who shined as big as starlit diamonds.

With that thought, he felt more calm. By the time he went back to his room to change into his comfortable clothes, he felt so much better. He was in control again and that made him happy. He felt so good, he was whistling.

ARCHER'S VOICE ECHOED through the door. "Dinner's here. Come and get it."

"Be right there!" Melody took one more look in the mirror. Her hair wouldn't hold a sleek look in this climate, so she'd resorted to twisting the thickness into a rope and using a large comb clip to clamp it on top of her head. Long tendrils hung around her face and her bangs swept just right to one side. Her makeup was flawless, looking as if she barely had any on when in truth it took lots to look like that. But there was no denying that plaid pajamas were plaid pajamas. If she'd had any sense at all, she would have seen this evening coming and prepared better for it!

"Melody? Are you okay?"

"I'll be right there!" She gave one last tug on the cranberry-and-green flannel pajama top that came to just above her knees, and straightened the solid cranberry bottoms so the folding seam looked straight. Then, as if marching to her death, she walked into the living room.

A warm fire crackled, old rock music played softly in the background, and the sexiest man in the world sat on the couch staring into the flames, their golden shadows dancing on his blond hair and contrasting with his gray sweatshirt that was artfully torn at the neckline. Very manly, rugged and…dangerous.

There was that word again. She thought of it often when she was around Archer. Come to think of it, even when she wasn't around him…

His gaze darted to her, locking with her eyes and holding her in place. She had an almost overpowering urge to run and curl up beside him, her bare feet between his body and the cushion. She wanted to wrap her arms around his waist, rest her head against his chest, hear his strong, steady heartbeat.

But her stomach reminded her loudly that she wanted to eat first.

"Darn stomach."

Archer grinned boyishly as if he knew exactly what her dilemma was. He patted the couch. "Sit down and eat, woman. We've got the evening to ourselves, and we might as well enjoy the hell out of the peace and quiet. This is better than being at home with the television blaring, the phone ringing every five minutes and women—Well, it's lots quieter."

"Heck, that sounds a little like fun." She sat down beside him. To her, this was far more exciting than home. Home was dull and boring. And quiet. Peaceful. A good place to raise a child....

He didn't answer, just gave her a look that said, "are you kidding?" and went back to the trays, lifting each metal top to show the food underneath. "You ordered a fruit salad, and I ordered a steak-and-lobster-tail plate with a baked potato," he explained as he lifted more tops off more plates. "And then I thought that since you were so diet conscious, maybe you would revel in Alaskan king crab legs dipped in lemon and garlic butter. It's something you wouldn't ordinarily do, and that's what this weekend is all about, isn't it?"

He got this weekend right. Just sitting here was something she didn't do!

Her mouth watered at the crab legs. How did he know? Her eyes narrowed on him. "You didn't do this out of the goodness of your heart. What's the real reason, Archer?"

He looked too innocent. "What do you mean? I just thought you'd enjoy them. I thought it'd be fun for you. That's all." Innocence turned to hurt that she would suggest such a thing.

But she wasn't buying it. Her father used to get that look when he was trying to hide the results of his imagined big picture. There was more to this and she wanted to know what before they went any further.

"Truth," she stated stubbornly, not letting him off the hook.

"Damn, lady. You're persistent."

"Truth," she repeated.

Archer sighed heavily. "Okay, okay. I'm having lobster in butter-and-garlic sauce. The only way I can have that and kiss you to distraction later, is if you have some, too. That way, we'll both have garlic breath."

Melody stared at him a moment, her gray eyes wide. "That's ingenious," she said.

He smiled, suddenly looking bashful and proud at the same time. "Thank you."

"And I love crab legs," she added truthfully.

"Then eat up, my lady. Before our drawn butter gets cold."

So, with soft music playing in the background and the hot tub's gardenia-scented steam hanging in the room, a fire blazing cheerily in the fireplace, and shadows swaying in the trees outside, Melody enjoyed every bite of her salad and crab legs.

"Um," Archer said, holding up a forkful of steak while he chewed on a piece. "Try this. It's delicious."

Obediently, she opened her mouth and accepted his offering.

"Great. I love a woman who does as she's told."

"Wonderful. I love a man who does the expected."

"Ouch. You aim for the ego, lady."

"Didn't you?" she asked, not letting him off the hook.

"No. I was teasing. You weren't."

His expression was somber enough to make her believe him. She felt guilty. She placed her hand on his arm. "I'm sorry."

His grin was as sexy as any movie star's. "Thanks. Now, open up again." He forked another bite of steak and popped it into her mouth.

She picked out a piece of her crab and dipped it into the butter sauce. "Taste," she demanded.

He did.

Archer told a silly female joke. Melody countered with a male-bashing joke. They kept on feeding each other tidbits of food. She had never done anything like it before and hadn't enjoyed anything so much. When she made him laugh, it was a balm to her ego.

When the plates were empty and her stomach was full, Melody sat back and gave a wonderful groan. "I ate too much and gained sixteen pounds in one hour."

Archer sat back and put an arm around her shoulders, giving a squeeze. "And it looks so good on you, too."

"You're just saying that."

He reached for a napkin and gently wiped a dribble of butter off her chin. "Yes. I'm just saying that," he repeated, his voice going lower.

He stared at her lips. Her mouth parted slightly and she watched Archer with eyes half-closed, her body humming with warm fuzzies. "I'm up here," she said softly.

He glanced up from her lips and met her eyes, looking like a little boy who just got caught.

"You're everywhere." He leaned forward, his mouth just inches away from hers. "Now, tell me. What is it you want to learn from me?"

"Learn?" Her mind was a blank. The only thing she could think of at this moment was that she was so thankful they had both eaten garlic! Then she twigged to what he was talking about. "You mean why I participated in the auction to begin with."

He stayed only inches from her mouth. "Talk to me. Tell me the biggest secret you've got." His smile was warm and confidential. "Come on, I won't tell anybody."

She thought of a hundred secrets—and a hundred reasons not to repeat them. "I don't have any secrets."

"Liar, liar, pants on fire."

She shrugged as if it meant nothing when it meant everything to her. "You already know my biggest secret. I need to know why men don't want to stay with me through to a marriage," she confessed. She'd told him before, she might as well admit it again. Somehow, it mattered far more now than it had ever before. "Help me understand what I'm doing wrong."

"What do you think you're doing wrong?"

"Don't play psychiatrist. Help me." It sounded more like a plea than a put-down.

Archer smiled, then sat back, giving her room to breathe. She sighed because she missed him at the same time that she was relieved.

"What did the last boyfriend say?"

"He said his new girlfriend needed him. And that I didn't need anybody." Talking about it was like reliving that confrontation all over again. "But I do. He just never saw it."

"Was she prettier than you?"

She blushed, but looked him straight in the eye. Did that mean he thought she was pretty? She was afraid to ask but wasn't afraid to give an honest answer. God only knew, she paid for this advice. "No."

"Did he go to her for rollicking sex?"

"No. She was too retiring to be a sex siren."

"Was she more of a clinging vine?"

"I'm not sure, but I think so."

"What is he like?"

"Jerry was sweet and retiring at home, but with a desire to make it to the top of investment brokering that superceded everything. He wanted me to become more involved in Junior League and join lots of clubs so I could tout his name."

"And you didn't want to?"

"No. I didn't mind, but I didn't realize how important it was to him. He mentioned it two or three times then let it drop without discussion. I just wasn't going to have it shoved down my throat. I'd had enough—" She closed up. Her family history wasn't the point of the discussion.

"Enough of what?"

"Of being pushed into things I don't want to do. My parents did it for years. As a matter of fact, they're masters at it. My teachers did it, too." She refused to tell him about all the private schools she went to because there wasn't someone at home to take care of her. It didn't matter how much she wanted to remain at home. They said no and that was that. "I want to do the things I want to do and still share my life with someone. I want a child to love and raise, and maybe a husband to care for. I want to walk next to someone, not follow behind where I can't see where I'm going."

"In other words, you know exactly what you want?"

"Yes." She closed her eyes for a moment, banishing the tears she knew were close to the surface whenever she thought of wanting a home to care for and a big family to love. "I just don't know if I can get it."

Archer's look softened and she could tell her emotions were showing more than she thought.

"Did any of the other guys tell you something or give you reasons before they left?"

"One did say I wanted a baby more than I wanted him. That was the last one." She gave a small, sad smile. "He was probably right."

"I won't touch that one. What else?"

"One said I wasn't responsive to him." That was hard to admit, but she needed to know the truth. Did every man expect a cross between a sex kitten and a firecracker all the time?

"Responsive?" His brows rose. "As in physically responsive?"

She nodded.

He came closer, stealing her breath away. "I

know you were responsive earlier this afternoon. But I don't want you to think I'm interested in a lifetime commitment if I kiss you."

"Don't worry. I promise I won't take you seriously."

He grinned. "Let's see how responsive you are now," he said in a husky voice.

His mouth very slowly covered hers, his touch so gentle she almost cried with relief. She'd been waiting all afternoon for another one of his kisses, tense as she waited. Now she was even more anxious because the moment was at hand and she wanted him to hold her so badly it made her hands shake.

Her fingers dug into his arms, as she pulled him closer. She wanted to do more than taste him. She wanted *him*.

His tongue danced lightly with hers, when she really wanted him to be forceful and lead.

He pulled away. "You seemed to respond well," he said, thoughtfully.

"Kiss me again, please."

He did.

Her head spun as this time his hands held her waist more firmly. His mouth was so pliable she sank her breasts into the hardness of his chest.

"Hmm. You're still responding just fine. I'm not sure I understand the problem," he said, pulling away.

Her breath was short, sharp and she didn't, couldn't reply.

He hesitated, giving something thought. "I'll try one more time," he whispered just before his mouth came down on hers. His hands slipped around to her back, pulling her to him. He was definitely in charge this time. Her hands slid up his chest and she held on to his shoulders, keeping him close to her. His chest brushed her breasts as he moved back and forth, teasing, tempting, inciting her nerves into a breakdown with her brain.

She was all feelings, all senses except the common one. She had been attracted to Archer from the very beginning, and now that she was in his arms, she knew why.

He led the way instead of waiting for her to lead. He was master instead of follower. He was...

He was unattainable.

When he pulled away, he cradled her head tenderly against his chest. Archer was much too handsome for the likes of her. She was nicelooking and a good person, but that wasn't his type. His type were models—tall and leggy models with gorgeous faces, thick blond hair and sexy eyes. Archer's women looked as if they knew what they were doing and could do it more sensuously than anyone else.

His kind read the latest books, knew the latest people up for their fifteen minutes of fame, were able to circulate at any party and command attention and adulation. His type knew what to say—always. His type was one of the beautiful people.

Melody was none of those things.

Before she thought, she spoke. "I'm sorry. This is a waste of time. This won't work."

His brows came together in a frown. He didn't let go of her waist. "What the hell are you talking about?"

Panic and fear filled her. She wasn't sure why or how, but she suddenly couldn't breathe with the thought of him leaving her. She'd leave first.

She took a deep breath to still the panic. "You. Me. This isn't working. I'm not your type. And I did this all wrong."

"How?"

"I don't know! I thought you could tell me what I'm doing wrong, but I don't think this will work. You're used to models and I'm just an ordinary woman. This was a bad idea."

"You're nuts," he stated calmly. "I'm turned on and you're blaming yourself for something I'm not even sure I understand. But you want to crucify yourself. I think I'm beginning to get the picture."

He was supposed to reassure her that everything was all right, not call her insane! She bristled. "And your sweet-talking ways are supposed to soothe and calm me? Is that it?"

He gave her a look that told her she was still insane in his eyes. "You get scared and begin to play martyr. I'm supposed to step in here and let you know you're wonderful. Then you can be reassured and continue to build your wall."

She looked at him, confused. "What wall?"

He gave her a look that called her question a fake. "You know the one. The *I'm-not-worthy* wall. The one that keeps the guys away because they finally begin to believe it and move on."

"That's not true."

But he wouldn't let it go, darn him! "Oh, yes it is. And sometimes it's hard for a guy to keep reassuring the little sweetheart that everything's all right. You know? Sometimes the guy wants to be misunderstood and not worthy and wondering and vulnerable. Sometimes, he doesn't want to lead. Sometimes he just wants to enjoy the moment and be, well, spontaneous."

Her irritation was quickly turning to anger. "Oh, really? And what about the woman? What if she doesn't want to be the mama all the time? What if she wants to pretend she's a sex kitten even when she's not? What if she wants him to take charge and act like a man should once in a while? What if she wants to be nurtured for a while instead of nurturing?"

"Then you take turns," Archer said calmly. "Nothing wrong with both parties taking turns."

Suddenly, Melody couldn't sit still. It was too uncomfortable and he was too close to being right. Not that she'd admit it. "Well, you're wrong. You're so far wrong, you're off-the-wall wrong."

Archer watched her with narrowed eyes. "And you'd rather be right than have a relationship."

She stared at him. Did he say what she thought he said? "A relationship with whom? You?" She raised her brows. "You don't even know what a relationship looks like!"

"I've got an idea. And because of that I'm not looking for one. I'll look for a lot of them instead." He grinned and she wanted to wipe the grin off his face. "You're the one who asked me for this weekend, darlin', not the other way around."

"You just think you're the answer to every woman's dream!"

A funny look came over his face for just a second. Then he reverted back to the Archer she'd begun to know—and like. Or used to until he started his pop psychology course on her!

"Melody Chase, every time you analyze me, you can expect the same. I'm a master at getting women to do what I need them to do for the success of my business. That's why you bid on me, remember? I know women and can compare experiences. You want to know what's going on in your relationships and I'm the one to tell you. But I won't do it if you're going to attack me for giving you the very information you requested."

He stared at her, his calm demeanor even more infuriating than if he had shouted. She wanted to hit him. To yell at him. To tell him where he could go with his information requirements and knowledge of women. But he was right. That was exactly why she was here.

Forget the short-term attraction with Archer. If she was ever going to find happiness with the man of her dreams, the father of her future children, she had to work on it now. With him.

Besides, she already had mucho money invested in him. It was time to give in. He was right and she owed him that much.

"I'm ready to listen to the man," she said with a smile that gritted against her soul like sandpaper. "Go ahead. Teach me tonight."

Archer shook his head, staying seated in the cocoonlike couch. "Melody, what a woman you are. I forgot," he said, slouching into the cushions and staring up at her. He wasn't at all intimidated by her reluctance. Darn him.

"Darn you," She picked up a pillow and walked around the room with it against her breasts like armor on a Viking maiden. He raised his brows in question and she still didn't know what to say. Suddenly she smiled. Tell him the truth. "I want to be angry, but I'm not sure why."

"Because I found your little secret out, that's why," he said smugly.

And he had. When he'd told her about her wall, she knew he saw far more than she wanted the world to know. "Maybe."

"No maybe, woman. I did. You wanted to keep the world at bay and pick out just a few people you want to let into your inner sanctum. And while doing that, you want to enjoy life and living and friends and all that sh...stuff."

"What's wrong with that?"

"Darlin', how does anyone get to know you?"

She stared at him for what seemed only a moment, but must have been much longer.

His smile faded. "If you don't say something soon, I'll know you just shut the wall down on me, too."

"If I had, you would have walked out of the room, Archer. You don't look as if you suffer fools gladly."

"I don't. But we're stuck here together, whether we like it or not, so we might as well like it." His smile was sweet and gentle, but not the look in his eyes. She suddenly felt as if she were surrounded by wolves, yet there was only one in the room.

He patted the couch. "Sit. Keep me company."

Her alternatives were few, and his gaze warmed her in all the right places. So Melody Chase did as she was told—just like the good girl she was.

5

ARCHER'S SWEET, drugging kisses created the most heady, addictive experience Melody had ever had. He slipped his arms around her, holding her securely against his hard chest, letting her hear his strong heart beating rapidly against her cheek. She smiled. She wasn't the only one experiencing a strong reaction.

In that split second, she made up her mind. All her life, whether she knew it or not, she had chosen men because they seemed to have what it took to make good fathers. Better fathers than her own. That had been her sole criteria for dating a man. Until this moment, she'd never realized it.

Never had she just let go and had a good time with a man without that fatherhood issue in mind. She had programmed herself for that. Cautious. Cool. Planning ahead. Never spontaneous.

But this time was different. Archer would make a lousy father. He was no good as husband material. He didn't seem to know the meaning of the word *commitment*, unless it was used in a business sense. He had no idea of marrying anytime, let alone now. But for once, she knew what she wanted. Really wanted, right this minute.

She wanted to make love with Archer. Nothing else. Just have him as a lover. Right now.

Archer pulled back. "What are you thinking?"

She smiled dreamily. "That you're more than I bargained for."

"An honest woman." His laugh was deep and slow. "I like that. What else?"

"I'm not thinking anymore." She looked up at him. "You'll have to do the thinking for both of us."

"Lady, you've never *not* thought." He stroked her back, soothing her waist before returning to her neck.

Forget the analysis. She wanted more. "Shut up and kiss me."

And he did. Again and again.

When he touched her breast, she felt the warmth of his hand. When he cupped her flesh, she felt the heat of him. And when she slipped her own hand up his shirt and rested against the lightly haired muscle definition, her heart skipped more beats than it was able to cope with.

She moaned.

He groaned.

Soon, Melody's clothing was off, tossed on the carpet and over the side of the couch. Archer's shirt hung from the lamp shade, his sweatpants were in a black puddle on the floor.

She curled in his arms, her body against his, filling his hard spots with soft curves. Pressure built inside her like the lick of a flame built into a forest fire.

She was naive to have believed she could play

with fire and not get burned. She was silly to think *dangerous* was only a word when it came to Archer. She was brainless to think she could match wits with this man and win....

He was prepared for lovemaking, just like she'd known he would be. According to Crystal he was a legendary lover, ready for anything, including tumbling Melody Chase on the couch.

When he entered her, she felt complete and heavy and full of need. A banquet was being served. His lean, hard form rocked above her, his mouth capturing every slight breath she gave, every heightened emotion that escaped on a sigh. His lightly callused hands sought her lips, her ear, cheek, tip of her chin, her slim throat. And then he dipped his tongue into the hollow of her throat.

She heard herself moan and didn't care. His touch was delicious.

"Keep it up, darlin'," he said against her skin. "Don't stop now. You're so close. So very close. I can feel you...."

Then suddenly she was *there*—right where he wanted her to be. Her body stiffened with the intensity. She heard his delight at her pleasure, but couldn't think past the feeling. She couldn't think at all. Her heart stopped, caught in her throat. Her pulse beat so quickly she thought she was going to die from the ecstasy he created as a gift for both of them.

Slowly, ever so slowly, she drifted down to earth and back into the room, her heart slowly coming back into her body, pounding heavily in her ears. Archer's weight was heavy, comforting, his body still moving, but now with more intensity, more structure. His thrusts were measured, his breath hot and labored until suddenly he joined her in the throes of ecstasy.

When it was over, Melody lay in Archer's arms and held on for dear life. It was her turn to soothe him. It was her turn to run her hand over his head and whisper sweet nothings in his ear.

"You're so special, you know that?" Her whisper was barely heard, but his heart slowed down. He stayed, resting his head on her shoulder, his mouth soothing her, his warm breath caressing her.

For one long moment, she thought she'd died and gone to heaven. For one long breath, she had found a contentment she'd never known before.

Archer lifted his head and stared down at her. His heavy-lidded, dark eyes were liquid chocolate. "Are you okay?" he asked.

She reveled in his concern. "Fine." She smiled and touched his cheek with a fingertip. "Wonderful."

He matched her smile. "Well, lady. I'd say that you don't have any problem in the lovemaking area."

She stiffened. "Was this a test?"

"And if it was?"

She couldn't describe the hurt his words caused. She sucked in her breath at the burn of it. "Then get off me now, Archer. I'd like to be able to slap your face good and hard, and I don't have any leverage here."

"And if it wasn't a test?"

"Then I want to know why you just made love to me."

"Are you always this analytical afterward?"

"No," she said, her voice firm and strong. "But I still want an answer from you."

His laugh was a low growl vibrating against her breast touching her deep inside. "I made love to you because you're sexy and exciting and very, very soft and feminine."

His words soothed as he listed everything she'd always wanted to be, but never thought she was or would be. But she still wasn't convinced. "You're lying." He wasn't getting away with patronizing her. She wasn't going to believe everything he said just because she was foolish enough to think there was more to their lovemaking than a physical response.

But that small kernel of hope was nestled deep inside her heart. Just maybe, he was telling the truth....

"Tell me more," she demanded.

He looked down at her, the laughter leaving his eyes. "You're beautiful, Melody Chase. I didn't know it in the beginning. I was too dumb to notice. Or I was used to just one kind of beauty; the kind to put on covers or place in ads. A different kind, not the only kind. But I know it now. I recognize the signs of a woman who is open and vulnerable and full of honest-to-goodness emotions."

"More," she whispered, her fingers trailing around the curve of his ear.

"And for whatever reason those losers left you, they were wrong. Not you. Not that I can see." His lips touched hers. "It's my honest, ten-thousand-dollar opinion."

She sighed, her mind easing from the doubts and problems around their lovemaking. "Thank you," she said softly.

He chuckled. "No. Thank *you*."

He picked up her flannel pajama top, handed it to her, then found his own warm-up pants.

She couldn't believe that in less than twenty-four hours, her life had changed so dramatically. She had a whole new outlook on men. She had never been carefree in a relationship; from elementary school on, her actions had been carefully thought out and weighed. This was a first—this meet-someone-then-make-love. But here she was, naked in a cabin with a man she barely knew. Yet somehow, she felt as if she knew him better than any man she'd ever met. It seemed the most natural thing in the world to slip back into her clothing with Archer sitting next to her. She stepped into her flannel pants and stood, making sure the legs slipped down.

When she looked up, she found Archer bare-chested, his back curved into the couch, watching her with an intensity that sent her blood back into a heated state.

She raised her brows, daring him. "Say it."

His smile was so sexy it sent her blood to pumping heavily again. "I was remembering what you looked like when I came in with your lunch this afternoon." His eyes touched her breasts, hesitated on her waist, then drifted down to the apex of her legs. "You rose from the water like a nymph, stunning the hell out of me."

"You surprised me."

He continued as if she hadn't spoken. "I hadn't expected the body of Venus with the sweetness of a Madonna. But in that one instant, that's what you were to me."

Her mouth was dry. "I didn't realize I stood."

"And I didn't realize you went back into the water until it was too late."

"Too late for what?" she asked.

His expression, so intense just seconds before, became dark, then distant. "Nothing."

"Too late for what?" she repeated, needing to know.

The distant look remained. "Too late for me to see everything you had to offer."

Confusion. He'd just taken her from a sensuous, full-blown woman to an object. She'd thought he'd seen her—inside her—and now suddenly, he was denying that. But she wasn't going to let him get away without an explanation. "And what was it you thought I had to offer?"

"A honey-sweet body."

Scrap the mind, apparently. She thought about objecting, but realized that he couldn't have been attracted to much else that soon after meeting her this morning. Wasn't that her own response?

But this evening. Well, this evening was different. He'd shown her his tender ways, his caring smile and his wonderful and sweet sense of humor. She was a sucker for honesty and humor.

"Thank you," she said softly, meaning it from the depths of her heart.

His surprised look was quickly covered up with a boyish grin. "You're welcome."

She turned and stared at the flames. More than anything, she'd wanted this ecstatic, private, warm, incredible evening to go on forever. But he was through. He'd gotten what he wanted and he was ready to move on to something else. Well, not this time. She was going to be the one who ended the intimacy. She'd walk away with her dignity, leaving him to ponder the meaning of *her* actions instead.

"Well, big boy, I think it's time we get some more wood and build the fire a little bigger. I brought a book I'm dying to read, and warming my toes while I read sounds like a great way to spend the rest of the evening."

Without looking at him, she walked to the sliding glass door, opened it and stepped out on the deck. It was like a blast of cold air on her soul, waking her up for a moment. It certainly closed off all thoughts of heated lovemaking. Momentarily, anyway.

"My goodness," she muttered, staring up at the star-riddled sky. She passed the wood and walked to the railing, holding on while she bent her head back to get the full effects of the marvelous show nature put on. The night sky looked like a black blanket studded with silver threads. There were so many millions of lights, she was stunned. Having lived for most of her adult life in New York City where the lights of the city blotted out the celestial sky, she'd forgotten how mesmerizing stars could be.

She felt rather than saw Archer come up behind her. He put his arms around her waist, letting her head rest on his still-bare chest. The warmth of his body against her back made her feel protected. His heated breath echoed in her ear. "Beautiful." It was a whisper that raced through her body.

"Yes."

"So are you."

She hesitated only a moment. He was certainly talking about her soul, not her looks. "Yes," she replied, needing to affirm her self-worth aloud. "So are you."

"Melody...." His voice drifted off.

But she heard the regret and knew she had to stop the flow of it. It would hurt too much to hear him say anything that might detract from their earlier lovemaking. This was a magical weekend. One she'd have forever in her memory and she didn't want it to be blurred by anything bad or awkward.

She turned in his arms and looked up at him, a provocative smile on her lips. "Thanks for such an...entertaining evening. You helped make me feel so special. But I'd appreciate your help for the rest of my problem. I still need to know what I have to do to find a relationship that will last with a man who's interested."

"In marriage," he said, filling out her sentence.

She nodded. "I guess. It would be nice to have a father for my child, but I'm not swearing it has to be marriage. I have my own money." She gave him a quick hug. "And your expertise can be such a big help."

His voice sounded distant, but his clasp was still intimate and caring. "Have you met the right man yet?"

She looked up at him and shook her head. "Nope, but I'm looking. He's around somewhere, and when I meet him I'll know it."

Archer looked just a little relieved. "I'll do what I can." He hesitated just a minute. "Why is a family so important? What has happened in your own family that you're so driven by this need?"

"I'm not driven. I'm a responsible, loving woman who is looking for a mate. You see, I have a job I want for the rest of my life. I help people every day, and every day is different, filled with challenges. But I don't work full-time and I don't have to. I love my life and want to add children to it. With or without a husband. I have a lot of love to give, and what I really want is a house full of kids. Some women are like that. I'm good with children. Really good. And I've decided that if I don't have one in a few years, I'll adopt. But I want lots of them." She hesitated a moment. "Or at least two."

"You're an only child."

"Yes. So are you."

"Yes," he said, his voice harder than it was earlier. "I liked it that way. If there had been more, my mother couldn't have managed. I'd have had to take care of them."

"And I would have loved to." Melody was quiet a moment. "Funny how two people can see the same set of circumstances in such different ways."

"True. That's the way things go. Meanwhile, let's just enjoy the rest of our time together."

"A great idea." She looked up at the stars again, then gave a delicate shiver. "But let's do it inside. It's too cold to enjoy the outdoors tonight." Forcing herself to slip out of his arms, Melody grabbed two pieces of firewood and walked back into the living room.

Archer followed silently, closing the doors behind him. He took the wood from her arms and placed it in the fire, stirring the embers with a poker and fanning the flames. Then, lost in thought, he leaned a hand on the fireplace mantel and stared into the flames. The flickering firelight cast a coppery glow on his skin.

Her heart stopped for just a moment as she reveled in the image. It was a picture that would remain in her memory for the rest of her life.

Part man, part animal, part beauty, part fierceness, part lone, part social, part giving, part taking. The epitome of maleness....

Archer.

It took all her willpower to turn away and reach for her book. She curled up in the corner of the couch and flipped on the dim lamp, purposefully staring at the type on the first page. But her eyes drifted to the man who stood at the fireplace, his golden skin shimmering in the low light. His concentration on the flames was trancelike—as intense as her concentration on him.

She forced herself to look back down at her book. It was one she had read and loved before and wanted to read again, but the words blurred together.

Melody's gaze drifted back to Archer. From any angle, he was beautiful.

Just at that moment, Archer looked up and his eyes locked with hers. An immense yearning spread through her and turned to liquid heat. Her thoughts shimmered with an undisguised want that she couldn't label. She passed it off as nervousness.

Archer stared back, silently telling her something she wasn't quite ready or smart enough to grasp.

"I'm going to bed," he stated abruptly. "Got a book I can read?"

Melody's heart sank. "There's another one on my bedside table. Help yourself." She pasted on a smile. "Sweet dreams," she said, pretending to make herself more comfortable. "I'm going to read here for a while longer. The fire's too nice to leave."

"Suit yourself." Archer's posture was rigid, his face a bland mask. "See you in the morning."

She refused to watch him. But she didn't read a word as she sat quietly and waited for him to leave.

Once he was gone, the room wasn't as warm,

the fire not so hot. The couch wasn't as cozy. She stared at the cushions as if she could see them making love earlier. It had been such a wonderful moment, and now it was as if they'd never been entwined in each other's arms, in each other's emotions....

Regrets filled her, but she wasn't sure what it was she regretted.

Perhaps she should have taken the lead and asked that he stay by her side. He might like a woman who took charge.

Maybe she should have laughed off the whole sexual episode, pretending that it meant nothing to her and that she had casual sex all the time. That lie might have eased the tension. It might have made him feel easier about sticking around for the evening. She might have been able to find her own sense of humor in the situation....

She stared at the page, forcing herself to concentrate. Ordinarily, she wouldn't have had a problem in the world. It was a good story by one of her favorite writers.

For now, though, she couldn't stop her gaze from straying toward the closed bedroom door. Every muscle in her body was tensed in fight-or-flight mode. More than anything else in the world, she wanted to walk into Archer's room and ask him to hold her. She wanted to curl next to his body, feel his arms around her and let the heat of him wrap around her. She wanted to feel secure and loved. And not so alone.

She sat up. Loved? Where in the heck did that

come from? Archer wasn't her type. Nope. Not at all.

Her soul mate was warm, funny and so much in love with her, he'd climb any mountain, cross any ocean to be with her.

That wasn't Archer.

The tension inside her mounted until she thought her shoulders would be permanently bunched up around her ears. She couldn't read. Heck, she couldn't even sit still. So she paced.

Melody walked back and forth across the living area, her feet keeping pace with her pulse, her pulse growing more rapid with each pass by Archer's door.

She wasn't knocking on his door. That was all there was to it. The pig. He'd made love to her and after she pulled away he was content to slip off to bed, satisfied. He was supposed to miss her. He was supposed to want her back in his arms.

Instead, she was the one with the problem, not him. Oh, not because his lovemaking fell short. On the contrary. She'd been satisfied so well that she didn't want the feeling to end.

That was the problem! She wasn't ready for this wonderful feeling to end. She wanted more. Her greediness knew no bounds! She wasn't content to spend the weekend with the most eligible hunk in the western hemisphere. Oh, no! She wanted him to make love to her all night, too. Afterward, she wanted him to hold her and talk into the darkness about all his hopes, dreams and ambitious plans for the future. She wanted them to fall asleep in each other's arms. And then, the next morning she wanted him to wake up and realize just how wonderful she was. Especially compared to all those other, more beautiful but less wonderful women who walked through his studio—and his life. She wanted him to say that again, and this time mean it.

"Yee Gads," she muttered, pulling back a strand of hair. "I *am* living in a fairy-tale world."

She glanced at her watch. It was past midnight and she wasn't the least bit sleepy. She had to do something or she'd be a wreck tomorrow morning.

Melody took action. She heated milk, poured it into a water goblet, then walked into the living room, stripped and stepped into the hot tub once more. Heat and steam swirled around her.

She sank even farther into the water, a sigh escaping her lips as the heat permeated her tense muscles and allowed her to relax, one inch at a time.

Lifting thick, dark hair away from her neck, she rested her head against the rim, then stared up at the ceiling and frowned. Surely, this would help her sleep....

Five minutes later, her nape began to prickle. She knew without Archer saying a word that he was in the room. She closed her eyes and ignored the fact that he was near. But her muscles refused to relax.

What was he doing? Why didn't he say something? Then she remembered. Her clothing was heaped in a pile on the floor next to the tub and she was now stark naked again. She felt onstage and awkward. This wasn't lovemaking, this was voyeurism. She wasn't confident enough to be stared at, veil of water or no. Her hand crept to the dials at her side and she switched on the pump so bubbles obscured her body.

Then she waited. Long moments passed by and still nothing. Cautiously, she opened one eye. Her breath caught in her throat. Archer was on the last step into the heated water. Naked. His hips at the same level as her head. No doubt about it, he was all male.

But she already knew that.

She quickly shut her eye, but now her heart beat so fast she thought he might think it was another pump displacing water. Her body wanted to soar with the bubbles, but she kept herself close to the seat. If she was wide-awake before she got in, she was wired now.

The last thing she expected was Archer's kiss. It started as a brush across her lips, and she thought it was one of the bubbles. It happened again, but this time it was just a little more defined.

It was definitely Archer. Her lips parted as he repeated the motion. Anticipation seared through her—anticipation of his kiss, his body, his presence. Everything that made Archer, Archer filled her spirit.

"You taste like gardenias," he said, his voice barely above the sound of the pump.

She opened her eyes to see him floating directly in front of her. "You taste like Archer."

"What's that like?"

She pretended to think. "Moonbeams."

His finger stroked her cheek. "You're so soft. Inside and out."

Her hand grazed his jawline, feeling the days' growth. "You're so hard."

He grinned wolfishly. "So glad you noticed."

She blushed. Darn it, would she ever get over that nasty habit? There was no sense in explaining her words. He knew she hadn't meant them that way...then again, maybe she had. "Why did you join me, Archer?"

"I couldn't sleep."

"Why?"

"Because you're in the water, naked. And I was in my bed naked. And it dawned on me that we had something in common."

"And?"

"And so I'd rather share my nakedness with you. Here."

She wasn't willing to let him off the hook yet. "Why?"

His look became playful. Wickedly male. "Because you're cute and sexy."

"And I'm here and available." Her voice was flat.

Archer tilted his head and stared down at her with a mischievous look. "We both are. What's wrong with that?"

What she wanted more than anything else was to be so important to him that he couldn't stay away from her. That he'd look at her and see a perfect wife and mother. Someone to revere. Someone for him. But she couldn't tell him that.

Instead, Melody smiled. "I think I'm tired now."

"Sleep with me?"

"Archer," she began.

"Just sleep. I promise," he said. "Honest."

She wanted that more than anything. At least for now. It meant that he wanted her in more than just a sexual way. "Okay."

Archer stood and held out his hand. His dark-eyed gaze was tender and sweet, touching her more than his sexy ways. "Come on. I'll help you."

With a sigh, she stepped out of the water after him. He tenderly wrapped her in a large towel then casually placed another towel around his own lean hips.

After turning off the spa and the lights, then checking the doors, Archer finally led her into his room.

In minutes she was in the big heart-shaped bed, curled in Archer's arms in the dark. His warm breath caressed her temple. She snuggled closer and his arms tightened. He kissed her cheek and his breathing was steady.

Melody smiled. Her eyes drifted closed and, within minutes, she was sound asleep.

6

WHEN MELODY AWOKE, she was alone. The
sound from the bathroom told her that Archer
was in the shower. Quickly, she slipped from bed
and ran into her own bathroom. Looking in the
mirror, she was glad she had. Her mascara had
run, making her look like a raccoon. Her eyeliner
was gone, and there was no highlighter left on
her cheeks or lips.

She took a shower in her bathroom in less than
three minutes, then dressed and put on makeup
in another five, breaking some kind of record.
She'd never gotten dressed in under ten minutes
in her life.

But then, she'd never felt so alive in her whole
life, either.

All the thoughts and worries that usually filled
her were pushed aside. She had the rest of her
life to rehash, relive and regret whatever she'd
done. She was good at that part. But not now.
Now she would enjoy the moment and bask in
being oblivious.

When she walked into the living room, she
was flushed pink from the effort and anticipation.

Archer stood facing the sliding glass doors,

staring out at the forest. A cup of steaming coffee was in his hand. A pair of faded jeans and a blue plaid shirt fit him well, shaping to his lean torso and accentuating his broad shoulders.

Although she hadn't said anything, he must have heard her entrance. Very slowly, he turned his head and stared at her without saying a word. The electricity between them was so strong it almost hurt her to connect with his gaze.

Memories of last night made her embarrassed and thrilled at the same time. Her gaze darted away, looking anywhere but at him. "Ready?" she asked brightly.

"For what?" His voice was soft, low, easy on the soul.

"For breakfast. Aren't we supposed to meet Shirley and Duane at the lodge?"

Archer took the last swig of his coffee and walked across the room. "I'm ready if you are."

They walked in peaceful silence down the path, hand in hand. They reached the restaurant all too soon.

Once they reached the table where Shirley was impatiently waiting, Archer changed completely. Not for the first time, she realized what a chameleon he was. He fit in anywhere. Whatever people needed from Archer, they got. Well, almost, she reminded herself. Just the same, there was more depth to him than she'd first assumed. More by far.

His sexy, little-boy smile was in place, the dancing light in his eyes glittered with hidden delights and unspoken messages. And his body moved as if it were fluid.

"Good morning, y'all. Hope you had a wonderful night's sleep and the day greeted you with a smile," he said, sounding like someone from the Deep South.

Shirley beamed in greeting. "Well, I hope you two had a nice evening. What did you do? Howl at the moon while no one was looking?"

Archer gave Melody a sideways glance and a wink. "Why, you might say that," he drawled.

Shirley laughed and Duane looked very interested. Suddenly Melody felt as if everything she and Archer had done was laid out on the table for everyone to see. Her blush began at her toes and went all the way to the top of her head. It didn't go unnoticed.

"My, my, a lovely time was had by all," Duane said, imitating Archer's drawl.

Melody shot Archer a look, then sat down, pasting a smile on her mouth. If he could carry this off without losing face, so could she. "My patron and I danced by the light of the moon. It was very nice." It suddenly sounded very boring. She had her dignity back, but she wasn't sure she wanted it.

"So," Archer said as a waitress sat a cup of coffee in front of him. "What do you want to do today that we can photograph?"

Melody turned her cup right side up so the waitress could serve her coffee, too, but the young lady never saw her....

She only had eyes for Archer.

As did Shirley.

As did Melody.

ARCHER'S GOODWILL was slipping badly by the end of the afternoon. They'd rented a car and gone on a shopping expedition in a quaint little German town. After posing by every statue, every little shutter-framed window and in front of every mural on the street, he was fed up. But the photo sessions hadn't worn on him as much as Shirley's incessant questions.

Especially on the way back to the lodge. Shirley knew this was probably her last chance to get the story, and she had a captive audience sitting in the back seat of the car. No one would make the mistake that she did this as a hobby. She was too tenacious.

"So, what is your first name? After all, no one's born with just one name, much as Cher would like you to believe it," she said with a smile.

"Archer is my first and last name, so I just shortened it to one name."

"Archer Archer?"

"My mom stuttered."

"I doubt that," Shirley said, her eyes narrowing. "Now tell me the truth."

"I just did, but the fact is I had my name changed to Archer legally." He gave a half-hearted grin. "So, you see, that really is my name."

"I bet there are plenty of women who'd like to be called *Mrs*. Archer."

Archer gave a deep frown at the memory of

some of the "women" who had fought in vain for that right. They had been more interested in status and money than in Archer himself. And although those were legitimate assets, they weren't enough to hold a woman to his side. Instead, he'd felt like some trophy to be won—or some fresh piece of meat on a runway. He'd had enough of that.

All his life, he'd wanted to be loved for what he was inside, not for how he was built or for his face or for how fat his wallet was. So far, though, not even his mama had done that. He sure as hell hadn't met anyone he loved and who loved him just for him in return. He didn't have a clue what love felt like. He was beginning to believe he might not ever know that.

"I'm too tough to work in tandem, Shirley. Some poor woman would never get her fair share of lovin' from the likes of me. So, I'm thinking that I'll just help all those single young things out by being there when they need a shoulder to cry on."

"Have you *ever* been married?" she persisted.

"Nope," he said with a carefree smile. All he wanted to do was get back to their cabin, sit on the couch and hold Melody. They had one more night together, and this was it. Why in the hell should he waste it talking to a woman he wasn't interested in talking to about a subject he wasn't interested in discussing?

"I'll tell you what, Shirley," he said, trying his best to keep a smile on his face. He had a feeling it wasn't working well. He put his arm around

Melody. "Some day I'll tell you all about it, but right now, I'm just happy and flattered to spend the weekend with such a sweet woman as Melody, here."

"Well, isn't it wonderful that she bid on you, then." Shirley's smile was as fake as his.

"Isn't it?"

Shirley's sharp gaze arrowed in on Melody. "So tell me, Melody. Why did you decide to 'buy' Archer here? I mean, I know he's gorgeous, but there had to be some other reason why you'd plunk down hard-earned money for a man you don't know." Her brows raised. "Or did you know him before?"

Melody leaned back against his arm, playing along. "I only knew Archer by reputation," she said softly. "But, being a professor who specializes in reading skills and since I teach reading to Spanish-speaking immigrants, the literacy charity is something I've always supported. And I happen to read Heart Books, so when I received the invitation, I knew I had to go and see."

Archer was surprised. He hadn't known she spoke Spanish, let alone that she taught people to read English. He'd underestimated the woman. There was more to her than met the eye.

"But you bid ten thousand dollars," Shirley stated.

"It was for a good cause." Melody slipped even deeper into Archer's sheltering arm.

Archer knew he should help her out by deflecting Shirley's questions, but he, too, wanted to hear Melody's answers. She was going to squirm for just a minute so she wouldn't have to tell Shirley the real reason; the intimate reason. The one that said *baby* and *sperm donor* in capital letters. He promised himself that he'd step in and rescue her if things got sticky. But for now, he'd allow her to answer. She was doing well so far. Besides, her edited version had piqued his interest....

Apparently it was Duane's turn to ask a question. "Do you always give so much to charity?"

"No," she gave a slight laugh. "Of course not. But this was a special opportunity."

"And why buy Archer?"

Archer hoped Melody could come up with a good answer. He was dying to hear it himself.

She took her time forming the words. "Because I thought he'd seen every beautiful woman New York had to offer, so he could relax with me and I with him."

But Shirley wasn't letting it go at that. "But why?"

Melody's lashes brushed against pale cream cheekbones. He felt the tension in her shoulders and knew that this was so hard on her. But she hadn't looked at him once for help so he was staying quiet until he felt she truly wanted him to step in.

"I thought he could explain the male mind so I could better understand." Melody said it simply and honestly.

Just from the look on her face, they knew it was the truth. Archer watched her every inflection. She'd been honest without giving away her own personal reasons for needing that information. She never mentioned marriage or children before thirty. She was good. He had a feeling she'd sidestepped questions before. She was very good.

But Shirley wasn't about to let it go. "Why would you care how the male mind works?"

Melody looked up, acting surprised and a little shocked at the question. "My goodness!" she said, a small knowing smile on her full lips. "With over half of the population being male, don't you think it'd be good to know how their minds work? After all, many of my students are male, too. And that doesn't count the university staff, my bosses, and half the people living in my building." Her smile widened into teasing. "Surely you'd like to understand the way their minds work. Sometimes men seem so…" she looked thoughtful and slightly flustered, as if groping for words. But Archer knew better. This woman was really, really good. "…difficult to understand without help or counsel from their own sex. Don't you think?"

Now it was Shirley's turn to look confused. Archer wanted to laugh aloud. Melody had successfully clouded the issue enough to deflect the fact she'd just paid ten thousand dollars for a man and a weekend in the Poconos. No one wanted to "understand" men that much unless they had money to burn. Apparently, she did. But he'd get to the bottom of that little puzzle later.

The laughter he'd felt earlier disappeared into

wondering. If Melody had snafued Shirley just now, could she have done the same to him? And if she had, what had been her purpose? Her *real* purpose? Ten thousand dollars was a lot of money to splurge just to get some information any college professor could have gotten from a self-help book....

The lodge was within sight.

Shirley and Duane would soon be a fragment of his memory of one special weekend—one in which he'd never had to work so hard for publicity.

As they drove up to the front of the lodge, Archer took Melody's hand in his in readiness for their getaway. When the car stopped, he opened the door and stepped out, pulling her with him. To hell with publicity. He'd done the whole damn thing and was tired of it. Right now, all he wanted was to spend time alone with Melody.

"We're taking a walk, guys. It was nice spending this time with you. Maybe we'll see you in the city someday."

Shirley looked startled as she turned away from the valet and hitched up her belted slacks. "Oh, but I thought we'd have drinks and dinner together." She was almost whining.

"Not tonight," he said shortly. "You just reminded me that Melody paid a price to be here, and so far, she's done more publicity for the charity than she has for herself. I have to leave before 6:00 a.m. tomorrow morning. I have a shoot in Connecticut. So tonight, I'm wining and dining her. Alone."

"Well, yes, but…"

Archer stepped to the back of the car, taking Melody with him. Her wide grin told him she was loving every moment of his plan. "We'll see you later," he said, heading out the side path of the lodge.

He glanced over his shoulder just once. Both Shirley and Duane were standing at the car, staring at them.

As they rounded a wooded corner, Melody laughed. The laugh became contagious, making Archer grin. His grin turned into a smile, his smile met her laughter.

It took minutes to recuperate, and when they finally did, Melody was holding on to his waist, her perfumed hair just below his chin, her delicate touch heating him through the cloth of his shirt. He felt so connected to the woman in his arms. They could have been on a desert island for all he cared. He was complete.

"Let's go," he finally said, kissing the tip of her nose and then turning toward the walkway. He reached for the small pack attached to the backside of his belt. Inside was the compact camera he used for casual shots.

"Where?" she asked, looking around at the various paths that branched off.

"Don't know. Don't care. Let's just get lost before the barracuda finds us."

And they did. Archer really didn't care. One path led to another and another, each a little more secluded than the one before until the path turned to…nothing. They were out of the lodge area and into the forest. Archer always knew where he was, but didn't give a darn how soon they got back. He snapped photos of Melody all along the way with one of his newer, pocket-size 35mm cameras he'd been wanting to try out. Some with the late afternoon sun behind, some with the sun warming her face. All of them looked beautiful through his lens. And with every two or three photos, he stopped to brush his lips across her kissable mouth.

Archer didn't know why he was feeling so damn good about life in general, but he was and he was going to enjoy the rest of the day to its fullest. Suddenly, everything seemed to be bigger, brighter, sweeter and smoother with Melody beside him.

He knew it wasn't love, although he certainly cared for her feelings. He knew it wasn't lust, although he could have taken her on any of the grassy slopes of the trails. He knew he wasn't trying her on for a long-term relationship, although he couldn't imagine ever being bored with her.

Archer shrugged. He didn't care why, he just wanted the contented feeling that filled him right now to last for a while. These emotions put everything in perspective: his work, his love life, his personal life, his friends. They were all important, but suddenly one didn't overcome the others.

By sunset, Archer led Melody back to the cabin, sat her in the porch swing and brought her a glass of crisp white wine. She was delighted and the warmth of her gaze and gentle smile showed it.

He felt as if he and Melody were bound together as conspirators against the big, bad press and people representing the auction. They were teammates struggling to have privacy and enjoyment without the whole world knowing every move they made. It was a good feeling, one that Melody seemed to share.

He hated to admit how much he'd changed this weekend. Almost as much as she probably had, only his changes were inside, not where she could see them and take note.

In a week or two, this time spent together would be just a memory and they'd both be neck-deep in their own lives. But he knew he'd look back on this time and grin at the partners-in-crime feeling. He'd said and done things this weekend that surprised even him. It was as if he could be as caring and gentle here as he wanted to be, because this wasn't the real world. It didn't make sense, but he was feeling good.

"You're so kind," she said softly as he leaned back in the rocker and propped his feet on the railing.

He remembered a few other, more graphic, descriptions of him by women. "Some wouldn't say so."

"I don't care what some say," she said, stubbornly loyal. "I've seen you in action."

He grinned. She didn't have a clue as to how mean he could be. He wouldn't have gotten far if he hadn't been on occasion. But that didn't mean he wanted her to see that side of him. She didn't need to know. "Thank you, ma'am."

"So what happens now, Archer?"

He didn't look in her direction. Instead, he pretended that the sunset had captured his attention. "Whatever."

"What does that mean?"

That feeling of contentment he'd been experiencing all day was fading quickly. "Nothing," he finally said. "What do you want to happen?" He was waiting for her to say the words that would chase him away. The words that spoke of commitment, of wanting to make this a lasting relationship, about how maybe he was the husband material she'd been searching for. The father of her children. He thought he'd been up-front about not being committed. He thought she understood that he'd never be attached to anyone for long. Damn. He hated to show his tough side tonight, but he would…

"Well," she said, shifting to place her legs up on the swing and watch him with eyes that didn't miss a move. "Aside from that sausage on a stick we had at lunchtime, I haven't eaten. One thing I like is an evening meal."

Archer looked at her, keeping his face as bland as he could although his heart was feeling light again. She was talking food, not commitment. She wasn't asking for anything other than directions on the evening's amusements.

He knew he liked this woman! "We're going to the lodge and dine in style then dance the evening away."

Her gray eyes heated his body in places he didn't even want to think about. "Really?"

"Of course. It's the least I could do," he stated modestly. And it was the least. She'd just paid ten thousand dollars and hadn't been out of this place for a romantic evening meal.

"I haven't danced in a long time."

He was surprised. Sure her girlfriend was an immediate attention getter, but Melody had a gentle sweetness to her that wrapped around a man like a blanket from home. And when she wanted to turn on the sexual heat, that sultry look in her gray eyes was the only match she needed to fire him up. "Why not?"

She leaned her head back and rested it on the chair. "Dates don't seem to want to do that anymore. It seems movies and plays are the way to go these days."

"And you don't like that?"

"Oh, no. It's fine," she protested. "It's just that I think there ought to be a variety, not the same thing every time. Most dates think if they spend money, they've done something special and deserve a reward." Her voice turned a little hard. "Or goods in exchange for goods."

Archer felt his own irritation rise. And, well, okay…maybe just a little guilt. He might have thought the same thing once or twice in his youth. "You don't say."

"Isn't that awful?" she whispered, her voice sounding so sad.

"Awful," he repeated. But suddenly he itched

to move, to hit someone. The problem was he'd only find that someone by looking in a mirror.

"Archer?"

"Hmm?"

"Do I look…easy?" Her voice was so soft, so vulnerable. "I mean, we've been so open this weekend, I was just wondering about a little more advice. You don't have to answer if you don't want to. I won't get angry."

He turned his head and stared into those wide gray eyes that looked so worried right now. "Not on a bet." He said it firmly and with conviction because he meant it, even though she looked like a cross between the girl next door and a sex kitten.

"You're sure?" Her voice sounded anything but sure.

She looked soft, sweet, wholesome. Her form was silky and well-filled out. She wasn't heavy, just not anorexic like the models he was usually around. She was gentle, frank and easygoing— again, unlike the usual women he filled his days with. They were paranoid, fearsome and competitive. Her touch was caring, sympathetic, affectionate and sensitive.

And she brought out feelings in him that he wasn't ready for and didn't want to acknowledge. He wasn't what she was looking for at all. And he didn't want to be, either. Looking away, he swallowed. "Positive."

She sighed. "Thank you."

"I don't know why you should care," he said through clenched teeth as he thought of other guys pawing over her. "Just tell those losers to get outta town."

She looked away. "I was just wondering."

"What would be your ideal date?" he asked, curious as to how she saw things.

"Just what you described. Dinner. Dancing. Lots of small talk and good company without off-color comments to let me know what the pay-off is expected to be at the end of the evening. Some of the supposedly nicest guys in the world come on like gangbusters once the date begins."

"Turds," he muttered and gained a grin from her. "Well, we'll see what we can do."

Her grin turned into open delight. "That would be different."

Silence drifted between them, but it faded back into an easy quiet. Companionable.

An evening breeze brought with it a little humidity. The scent of fresh pine and barely blooming wildflowers was strong in the air. Archer held his hands behind his head and closed his eyes. They had two hours to relax before dinner, and he hadn't relaxed in a million years. Not since he was around nine, when he'd begun scrambling up the ladder of poverty and competition. Hell, he'd never sat still for longer than an hour. He'd never slept longer than six hours at a stretch. He was breaking all kinds of habits this weekend.

This was the life....

MELODY COULDN'T BELIEVE how magical the evening was. If she'd never seen Archer until this very moment, she'd still have fallen in "like" with him. Heaven only knew, she'd fallen in *lust* with him from the moment they met on the cabin porch. That was a first for her, too, but she wasn't willing to share that tidbit of information with him. She wasn't even sure she was willing to acknowledge it to herself! It seemed so…so… lusty.…

The restaurant was formal and romantic. Archer's attentiveness made Melody feel like a fairy princess. Smiling waiters served food that tasted like ambrosia. Off to the side, a small four-piece band played songs she could actually dance to if given the chance! Lighting, wine, Archer—all was perfect.

Thank goodness her dress, a royal blue knit she'd worn at the conference earlier that week, fit the occasion, too. Archer wore a jacket and slacks with a pale blue shirt. His blond hair shone under the warm lighting, making him look even more handsome than usual. If that was possible.

It was the kind of night that romantic dreams were made of—and Melody was *not* going to pinch herself and wake up.

Archer's sexy brown eyes never left her face. "Have I told you tonight that you're beautiful?"

She felt the heat of his gaze and returned it with one of her own. "Yes, but I could stand to hear it again another five or six hundred times."

"That can be arranged, beautiful." He lowered his voice another rich octave. "Dance?"

Her heart fluttered like an uncaged bird's wings. "I'd love to." She rose gracefully, feeling as if she were gliding on air. He took her to the dimly lit dance floor in front of a huge stone mantel and a blazing fire.

She walked into the circle of his arms and knew heaven had a name. It pounded in a thick, heavy rhythm with her pulse. Archer. Archer. Archer.

His mouth was close to her ear and his light breathing stirred her hair. He wrapped his arms around her waist, holding her to him as if there could be no part of their bodies that didn't touch. She knew he would have done the same with any other woman in his life, but she felt so…protected. Cared for. Loved.

There was that word again.

Liked, she told herself, replacing that elusive word with one she could work with in this odd relationship.

"Lesson number sixty-two," he whispered in her ear. "A man loves it when a woman molds to his body."

She lifted her head slightly. "Am I doing that?"

"Yes." His arm tightened, bringing her even closer.

Normally, she would fight anyone holding her this way. But not now, not with Archer. Instead, she snuggled right in, reveling in the warmth of his body, the tightness of his grasp. But most of all, her ego needed, basked in, his open display of attraction. It soothed the hurts of the past years' relationships and the fear that she wasn't feminine, not nice enough, not worthy as a lover…not worthy of a man.

But there was no doubt that Archer was all man. His body was tough, muscular, and so very pleasing to the eye. And very hard. All over. But there was a lot more, inside, that made Archer a man.

She was proud to be with him, proud of the physical need in him that she inspired.

The song came to an end and so did their dancing. Archer led Melody back to the table, where he plied her with another glass of Merlot, a giant chocolate-wafer dessert and two forks.

He told jokes, they laughed, they fed each other and laughed some more. And then Archer held her in the security of his arms, giving her looks that melted her heart and turned her body into a puddle.

When the waiter asked if they needed anything, Melody looked up for the first time in an hour. She was amazed to find they were the last ones in the restaurant area.

She was Cinderella—only she was the last one to leave the ball.…

The bandleader, taking in the scene, called a brief conference with his players then announced they'd play one last song. Archer stood and reached for her. Melody placed her hand in his and they walked to the dance floor. Encircled in his arms, she danced as if this night would never end. And it wouldn't.

For as long as she lived, she'd remember these enchanting hours with Archer. This would be a jewel in her mind's eye, a memory she could pull out any time in her life and relive the magic of being with him, even for a little while.

As always, he read her mind. "This isn't the end of the evening, Melody. There's more to come."

THEY STROLLED BACK to the cabin guided by a bright ribbon of moonlight peeking through the trees. Melody, loving the song they'd last danced to, hummed it softly all the way back. Archer held her hand securely in his, not leading, not following—just walking by her side. She wished this night was something that could last forever. But she knew better. These few moments were all she had. Still, she'd be darned if she was going to spoil it by feeling sad.

When they reached Archer's room, they stared silently at each other in the moonlight. The heart-shaped bed looked even larger in the dark than it did in the light.

Melody began the slow ritual of undressing, moving as if the music still played to a slow dance with magical movements. Though she knew exactly what was coming and anticipated Archer's lovemaking, she refused to waste any precious moment in haste. She removed each article of clothing slowly and deliberately, feeling as sensuous as she'd always wanted to be but never felt she was. Until now.

Archer's dark-eyed gaze was like warm, thick

chocolate, making her feel secure, more confident with each move she made.

By the time she stood in front of him naked, his eyes had floated over her body, warming each intimate place he touched with his gaze.

"Now for lesson seventy-three," he said, his husky voice a mere growling whisper.

Her eyes widened as she looked up at him. She placed her hand on his chest. "I can't even remember lessons one and two!"

"Lesson two was a snap. You made an A— passed with flying colors. The lesson was making the man you were with feel like a hero while he wines, dines and dances you through the evening." His fingers soothed her cheek, gently brushing a wisp of dark hair behind her ear.

It took a moment to find her voice. "And I did that?"

"Yes." Archer placed a kiss on her nose, his hand cupping her neck in a delicate hold. "And you passed lesson one, the social calendar dos and don'ts for dates. You were still so sweet after we left the 'pressing press behind,'" he said.

Melody placed her fingers over his lips as he spoke. "Shh. Don't speak disparagingly of them. They were only doing their jobs." She replaced her fingers with her mouth, tasting his lips with soft little sipping motions.

Archer groaned. "And I can tell already. You're gonna pass the next test with flying colors...." he said, his voice a mere rasp.

He quickly stripped off his clothing and then stood in naked splendor watching her with eyes that spoke volumes. As a fantasy, she couldn't have asked for more. To know firsthand what an incredible lover he was and to be able to stare at him—beautiful, naked—was the height of sensuous luxury.

Her own low laughter sounded triumphant as he held her close and made love to her as if she were the most treasured thing in the world. And she was sure that, for this moment in time with Archer, she was....

THE BED'S MOVEMENT and Archer's kiss on her forehead forewarned that he was closer than a breath away. Very slowly, she opened her eyes and blinked several times.

Fully dressed, Archer was seated on the edge of the bed, his arm braced on the other side of her body as he stared down at her. There was no smile in his gaze, no joke just about to be related. There wasn't that feeling of humorous, us-against-them feeling. There was just an honest look. She knew what he was saying. Silently, he was saying goodbye.

Her heart hurt from the effort not to cry.

Instead, she put on a smile and reached up, feeling his clean-shaven jaw. "You're leaving," she said softly.

"Yes." He twisted his head just enough to kiss her palm. "And I couldn't leave without thanking my partner-in-crime for a wonderful weekend."

"Thank *you*."

He stared into her eyes, his questioning. Finally he spoke and her heart raced in reaction. "May I call you sometime?"

"Anytime."

"And you're not, uh, with someone," he said, as though seeking confirmation.

"If I was, I would never have gone to bed with you, Archer. There's no one else."

He cleared his throat. "I don't mean we should be a couple. You know that. But, you do have a photo shoot coming with this package. And I thought maybe we could get together for a meal, or a movie, or something."

"I'd love to. You have my address and number. From that first night. Remember?"

He returned her smile quickly before getting to his feet. "You're a special woman, Melody Chase. Thanks for letting me play the knight in shining armor without the happily-ever-after stuff."

Her chuckle was low and throaty, but she couldn't voice aloud what was in her heart. "Don't worry, Archer. I won't hold you to it."

"I know. That's what was so much fun about it."

"I'm glad. Be safe."

He bent down and gave her one more kiss, but this was on the mouth, in the bed, and it took her breath away.

"Take care, Cinderella. See you soon." And then he was gone.

She leaned back against the headboard and looked around. They'd made love and talked far into the night. It was all small talk, intimate conversation that made her feel closer to Archer than she had ever felt to anyone in her whole life.

Now there was no physical trace of Archer. Oh, there was that unique, wonderful scent of him on her pillow and clinging to the bedsheets. Also, the side of the bed he slept in was still mussed. And she was sure that the bathroom still held wet towels from his shower and shave.

But there was nothing else; no luggage, clothing, personal items. Not that he'd left like a thief in the night. He'd whispered goodbye to her in the early morning dark as she was snuggled close to his body, encased in his arms. And he'd said a more formal goodbye just now.

She knew better than to ask him to stay. The lodge limo was waiting to whisk him away to his shoot in Connecticut. But it was the hardest thing she'd ever done. She had to bite her lips to keep from begging.

But it was over.

Time to go home and start hunting for a husband and father for her yet unborn child. Nothing had changed, she told herself. She still had her goals—they had been delayed for a week due to intense education. But she had learned what she'd set out to learn.

Melody stared up at the light fixture as dawn stole into the room. Archer's face danced in front of her eyes. Archer—holding her, touching her, kissing her, talking to her, making love to her.

She blushed with the thought of it.

It was over far too soon. Her heart sank to the ground.

Archer had had a good time—found a fun mate for three days and got publicity for his business. Not bad for a weekend's work.

It wasn't his fault that Melody had changed her mind about what she wanted from the weekend somewhere along the way....

She glanced at the clock next to the bed. It was time to go home. Her car needed to be returned to the rental company. Besides, she had a night class Tuesday for which she still had to prepare a study plan.

Sunrays peeped through the curtains in a bright thread, reminding her of the day outside. Leaves danced and dipped against the window, calling to her. Except she didn't feel like walking along the paths to the waterfall without Archer.

CRYSTAL LOUNGED ON Melody's couch, glancing though a fashion magazine, stopping at the page held with a Post-it note. Melody had marked Archer's photos. "Why not join a dating club?"

"No way. I'm not going to be asked to show credentials, then be poked and prodded to see if I'm ready or not." Melody gave a final stroke of coral polish to her baby toe and studied it.

"Then what, Melody?" Crystal persisted. "Archer tells you that you've got all the right stuff, and you're still hanging around waiting for Mr. Right Genes to come to your door unannounced." Crystal pitched the magazine on the coffee table, where there were more piled. "What's wrong with this picture?"

Melody gave a heavy sigh. She didn't want Mr. Right. She wanted Archer, who was all wrong for all the right reasons. It was that simple. "I want to be a mom, Crystal. It's an ache inside me that I can't assuage with other things, like ice cream or exercise. It's just that it would be nice to have the father of my child be my husband, too."

"I don't get it," Crystal said. "You've still got at least fifteen years to have a child, if that's what you want to do. Why now?"

How could she explain to someone who didn't have the same urge to give, to nurture? All she could do was try. "I grew up an only child, playing with dolls. They were my companions and best friends ever since I can remember. When I was old enough to relate to real live babies, I was fascinated from the very first one I saw." She remembered back, seeing babies in the park when she was taken there to play on the swings. "Babies fascinated me in the same way little boys become attached to trains, guns or baseball cards. And sometimes, they carry that into adulthood. That's what happened to me. I learned everything I could about children, I baby-sat constantly. At college I even got a teaching degree for primary school. But I also realized I'm a good teacher for adults, so I went in that direction instead. I knew that some day I would have children of my own, which would satisfy that part of me."

Crystal's eyes widened. Melody had never talked so openly about this before. She had never forced herself to think of the whys and wherefores until now. Crystal had done it again: made her think.

"I can't remember ever even thinking about wanting children," Crystal said. "But maybe it's because I was raised in Michigan with six brothers and sisters. There was nothing new or mystifying about kids. You had them and took care of them and occasionally wished you didn't have to do either one."

"Well, it's different for everyone. But for me...I've got a job, which I love, a home, which I love, a life, which I love...none of which are quite complete without a family to love. I'd be a good mother. I don't want to wait until I'm older. I want to enjoy my children and grandchildren while I'm still young."

"Well, you're a better woman than I am, Melody Chase."

"Not really. I just want something different. Children. Preferably with a husband." But she hadn't been able to get Archer off her mind long enough to even think of allowing another man into her life—and certainly not into her bed! "I can do without the man as long as I can have the child."

That sounded good, but she knew better. She knew what her problem was. She was head over heels, deeply in love with Archer. Love had happened quickly, quietly, stealing up on her when she least expected it—in the Poconos with a paid escort.

"Melody?" Crystal's voice broke into her thoughts.

"Yes?" She tried to shift her attention back to her friend. After all, she'd invited her over for a girl's night in, the least she could do was stop drifting away on thoughts of Archer.

Crystal gave an exasperated sigh. "Okay, so what happened with your parents today? Did they read you the riot act again? About the ten thousand? Is that why you're so far away?"

Melody capped the polish. "Of course. Mom and dad did their usual. Luckily, Dad's in the middle of some merger and Mom is planning her next dinner party. They can't get preoccupied with hitching me up to some nice boy they want me to meet."

Crystal grinned and piled her long, blond hair on top of her head. "As opposed to the last one who just wanted to pretend to like children so he could have your dad pay the bills."

"Oh, that's right. You met him." Melody sighed.

Crystal nodded grimly. "Your parents are the only people in the world who have found at least twenty genetically perfect males for their only daughter to mate with."

"As long as I promise not to enjoy it," Melody reminded her.

"Correct." Crystal smiled widely, showing perfect teeth. "Think of the flag and Mother Nature, or the color you want to paint the bedroom. You'll do fine."

"Come on, Crystal," Melody said as she stood

and hobbled to the chair in order to keep the cotton balls between her toes while the polish dried. "Think of another solution." She thought of Archer, but she wasn't naive enough to believe that Archer wanted the same things she did. That was an impossibility.

"Adopt."

It wasn't as if Melody hadn't thought of that before. In fact, she'd thought of it a lot. After all, single women could adopt now. And she had a lot of love to give. It wasn't as if she had to have her own genes so much as have a child she could love and who would love her.

She shrugged. "Why not?"

"You'd do it?"

"I don't see any reason not to. I have a good income, lots of money in the bank. I'm stable. I own my own place. And I want a child."

And she might as well face it. It was silly to wait around for Archer to come to his senses and choose little Melody over all the long-legged, thin, beautiful models he worked with in exotic locations all day, every day of his professional life. He'd made it pretty clear that he wasn't the serious kind. He'd never pretended otherwise.

On the other hand, she couldn't imagine being with anyone else. This was just a mind game to play so she could pretend she was still looking for the perfect man. The joke was on her; she'd already found him and he'd turned her down for…for all the other choices.

Crystal interrupted her thoughts. "I still think you ought to look for a husband."

"Where do I look?"

"Attica."

She gave the state prison a moment's consideration. "Somewhere else." She would never love again, but surely she could be a good wife and mother without swearing undying love between her and her faceless husband-to-be. She still had strong morals, and devotion was one of them. And no one could tell her that marriages weren't made for just these reasons. She wasn't the only woman in the world who was looking for a mate to begin a family. It was the most fundamental of all instincts.

Crystal thought for a moment. "A friend of mine is attending a publishing party. Wanna go?" She studied her own toenails. They were perfect, as usual. She had hers done by a professional. Melody refused to spend her money that way, although, heaven only knew, she had enough of it to spread around.

"Sure."

"Good, it's Thursday night. Be ready by five-thirty."

"Why so early?"

"It's a publishing party. They start right after work."

"And then?"

Crystal shrugged her feminine shoulders. Everything she did was feminine. "I don't know. It should last awhile, then everyone goes their own way."

"What's the party for?"

Crystal gave her one of those aren't-you-

ashamed-of-yourself looks. "Honestly, Melody.
You always have to know the details. Can't you
just trust in the process?"

"In other words," Melody said dryly, "you
don't know what happens next."

"Right."

"What do I wear?"

"Anything from business suit to spiffy cocktail
dress." Crystal took the small bottle of topcoat
out of Melody's hands and began applying it to
her own impeccable manicure. "And then, for
your birthday this weekend, we'll go to that new
club on the top floor of the publishing house on
Sixth Avenue. There's sure to be some wonderful
eligible bachelors there."

Archer popped into her head again. He had
done that like clockwork every five minutes since
he'd left her side last Sunday morning. She dis-
missed him, unwilling to get into a crying patch
in front of Crystal.

"Friday or Saturday?" Melody asked as if she
were interested. Nothing could have bored her
more—except maybe Attica.

"Let's set it up for Friday. That way we'll still
have Saturday evening open in case something
works out."

Fat chance. "Wonderful."

In the back of her mind was the thought of quietly flying off into the sunset. Maybe to Cancún.
"Maybe I'll go to the Caribbean," she mused
aloud. Dreaming of basking in the sun made her
feel pampered. She knew she wouldn't do it, but

the thought cheered her up a little. She could if she really, really wanted to....

When the phone rang, she felt more cheerful than she had since Archer and the Poconos.

"If this is the sweet and wonderful Melody who has a birthday coming up, say yes softly into my ear." Archer's voice sounded even more sexy than she remembered.

Her heart rose to her throat. "Yes," she whispered. "How did you know?"

"I have a great memory. You told me your birthday was just around the corner. You're going to be twenty-eight. Right?"

"Yes."

"Mmm, I love that word," he said with laughter in his tone.

"I'm glad. It's one of my favorite, too."

Crystal's brows rose.

"In that case, could I tempt you with a romantic dinner, wine and a view of the city?" His voice was whisky-rough and dangerously soft.

Her heart jumped up to her throat. Was he kidding? Of course... "Why?"

That got him. Obviously he wasn't expecting a question. He spoke slowly, patiently, as if talking to a child. "Why? Because I just got back from the New England shoot, which took a week out of my life. And I haven't seen you since I left."

"I thought you forgot." It was a simple declarative sentence that said so much more than she wanted to say, but it slipped out.

"I could never do that, Melody. It was a great

weekend and I've never been so relaxed with a…friend, before."

At least he called her a friend. It wasn't as good as some of the other names she could think of, but it was a start. "Neither have I."

"I want to see you for your birthday and this seems the way to do it. I guess I could come over, knock on your door and ask you to turn around a few times so I could get an eyeful, but I've been reading your favorite books.…" Satisfaction laced his voice. "I started with the one you had in the Poconos, and I've read a couple of others since."

She hated repeating herself but had no choice. "Why?"

"Because I wanted to know what a woman wants in a man. Now I know."

"And it is…?" she asked. Crystal's ears perked up. Her friend made a pantomime of asking who was on the phone. Melody covered the mouthpiece and whispered his name. Crystal made a victory sign and listened to each and every word.

Archer's voice was low and sexy in her ear. She tingled all the way down to her toes, with a few well-warmed spots along the way. "Well, he's more verbal than I thought. He's a man who knows what he wants and demands his partner be an equal."

Melody raised her eyes to heaven. "Thank you for someone getting the message."

Archer's laugh was low and easy. "So. What do you say? Dinner and the sights?"

"I'd love to. When?"

"Tomorrow night. Seven-thirty. We'll meet at my studio."

"Fine," she said, both hands holding the phone as if it might slip away. "Do you want me to bring anything?"

"Your lovely body. But if that's not available, I'll take your quick mind and delightful smile."

She sent him the latter over the phone. "In that order?"

"It wouldn't be very heroic of me to say no, would it?"

"No, but it might be honest."

"I'm honest, Melody Chase." He said it with enough conviction that she believed him. "Most of all, with myself. And certainly with you."

She didn't know what else to say. Her insides were turning cartwheels. "See you then."

"Goodbye, lovely Melody," he said, then the phone went dead.

Melody had trouble unclasping her stiff hands from the phone. She slowly lowered the receiver to its cradle.

"So?" Crystal's voice broke into her jumbled thoughts. "What did he say? When are you going to see him again?"

"How do you know I'm going to see him?"

Crystal gave her friend an exasperated look. "I heard half of the conversation, girlfriend. And the other half I made up. So fill me in on the details. Now."

Barely able to contain her news, Melody did.

Crystal gave a smug smile. "I knew I'd picked the right one."

"I agreed with your pick," Melody pointed out.

"Yes, but now you're on your way to the romance you always wanted to have with the man you're really in love with. That ought to be worth a trip to the Caribbean, don't you think?"

Melody ignored the word *love.* She hadn't said *that* word aloud, to anyone. She wasn't starting now. "For whom? You, me or Archer?"

"All of the above." Crystal looked smug.

Melody laughed for sheer joy. She didn't know if what Crystal was saying about Archer was true or not, but the fact that he wanted to have her for dinner—correction—have her *over* for dinner, left her happy beyond belief and breathless. And wanting to do something special for Crystal.

"Okay, if we can find a special package. Cheap."

"I accept with undisguised enthusiasm," Crystal said, not bothering to contain her feelings on the matter. "And anytime you need my advice on men again, please feel free to come to me. I aim to please all my customers."

Melody was ecstatic. Now, if she could only keep her mind on the everyday problems at hand until the next time she saw Archer....

ARCHER'S MAID LEFT at five-thirty. The take-out restaurant had delivered a banquet a little over an hour ago and it was ready to heat up. Melody would be here in half an hour.

He had tied several bright-pink balloons to the

dining chairs. There was gold and silver confetti scattered around the tablecloth.

And in the bedroom was a small square package containing a porcelain statue of a cherub holding a bow and arrow…something to remember him by.

Taking his time, Archer poured himself a glass of wine and looked around to make sure everything was in place. As always, he marveled at the perfection of his home. Of course, it was just one of the trappings of success—part of an image that had done well for him.

It had taken him a long time to get as far as he had, one expensive piece at a time. Now his apartment, his studio…his life, were exactly the way he wanted them.

If someone had told him when he was a kid on the street that he'd be living in a setup like this, he'd probably have punched them in the nose for lying. Yeah, he'd come a hell of a long way in a short time. And it was a short time. Some of his peers in this business were in their fifties and sixties and hadn't yet earned the reputation he had for quality work.

What he was most proud of was that he'd done it all on his own. There were a few people who had helped him along the way, but for the most part he'd helped himself by studying, hard work, long hours and dedication.

Archer sipped his wine. Wonderful furnishings in leather and heavy plaids, a great space for some of the photographic art he'd begun collecting recently—all paid for. All this, overlooking the East River and the sunrise....

Melody ought to be impressed.

Archer frowned. Melody was an enigma. He hadn't been able to get her off his mind since he'd left her in the Poconos. He hadn't really meant to contact her again. At least, not so soon. When he'd left that morning, he'd thought all he was feeling was regret that a vacation was over and relief that it had been so painless. In fact, he'd actually enjoyed his time with Melody— okay, more than enjoyed. But, right after he left, he didn't give it much thought as he tried to make all his connections and get cameras and film through the X-ray machines at the airport.

But every time he turned around, the ghost of her was there. Once he got home, he sat and grinned just remembering the times they'd shared. He hadn't realized just how insidious memories were. Within hours, they had taken over his life....

Melody had managed to invade his every dream, creep into his every thought. A model with knowing eyes had come on to him during the shoot in Connecticut, and he'd turned her down quicker than a second thought. He didn't want any woman—any woman except Melody.

That was certainly different. The women in his life had taught him never to rely on them, starting with his alcoholic mother.

He remembered coming home from school every afternoon to find her drunk or hungover. She would drink a pot of coffee and be full of repentance. But after working as a coin-girl all night at one of the gambling casinos, she'd come home and need a drink to "wind down." She'd wind down until she was passed out on the couch. Archer would cover her with a faded blue blanket, make his lunch and go to school. It would start all over again the next day.

His mother was sure that someday soon, "anytime now," she used to say, a wealthy man would walk through the casino doors, take one look at her and say, "Woman, I want you for my wife." And then they would all be on easy street, enjoying life. For a while, a very short while, Archer even believed it himself. But that hadn't lasted long.

His aunt would come to visit, and she'd storm and strut and cry over Archer. Then she'd sit down and get as drunk as her sister. Archer hated those visits. It meant he took care of two women instead of one.

When he went into photography, the models he worked with had a similar mentality. Everyone was absorbed in their own lives, there were no other problems but theirs. He learned how to play the game and make them believe he cared so much he bled for them. They knew better, but he got a product he was proud of and they got a paycheck and a better reputation.

Until the weekend in the Poconos, he hadn't bothered to take the time to realize there might be different kinds of women. He certainly hadn't run into them. Society parties were just older, richer models on the arms of older, wealthier men. Their self-absorption was the same.

Melody was different.

She blushed, she was modest, she made love with enthusiasm not with jaded experience. She was tender, had a wonderful sense of humor and used it, and was as sweet as his mother had been sour.

The memory of Melody had hung with him the entire time he was in Connecticut. He had expected to think of her, but he hadn't expected to dream of her, or wish for her to be walking by his side, sharing light secrets.

He hadn't expected to like her so damn much.

When he returned from New England, he'd looked up Melody's address and found it to be a very nice area on the East side, not far from him. Her inheritance allowed her to live there, he assumed. A college professor didn't do badly, but it wasn't the highest paying job around.

When he called and heard her voice on the other end of the line, he didn't care how different her life-style was from his. He was happy again. Looking forward to something. Enjoying something. Feeling contented outside of his career.

Why, even developing the film he'd shot of her on the trip had been a sad affair until now. Now he looked at the contact sheets and remembered each moment with a smile instead of regret. The whole scene came back vividly. Her comments, her smiles and laughter, her openness and delight with nature and just being with him—it all came flooding back.

Those photos were stuck on the walls of his darkroom, each one a gem. She wasn't the model type, but she *was* an angel. Her tawny skin, heart-warming smile and incredibly intimate gray eyes reached down to the very core of him, touching him in a way he wasn't sure he understood or wanted to. But it made him realize just how much he yearned to be with her again.

With her, he felt like one of those damn heroes she liked to read about. He felt big and tall and powerful. He also felt happy and full of fun, like the little boy he'd never been.

All those feelings were new to him and he wanted to feel them again. Most of all, he wanted to know if he *could* feel them again.

Part of him didn't believe it. Melody was no more real than the siren's song called to a sailor's soul.

When the doorbell rang, a glance at his watch told him that Melody was right on time. A smile began forming somewhere inside his chest, working its way up.

This was no time to stand on ceremony. Archer flung open the door and took her in his arms. Her wide gray eyes opened even wider in appreciation. He lifted her up and slowly swung her around, her delighted smile only inches from his own. Her perfume wafted around him, powerfully reminding him of how much he missed filling his senses with her essence.

"Hello, you sweet young thing, you," he finally said softly, letting her drift down the length of his body.

Her hands tightened on his shoulders and she caressed his face with her gaze. "Hello, you handsome thing, you."

He kissed the softness of her cheek. "I missed you."

She kissed him back. "I missed you, too."

He kissed the corner of her mouth. "I'm glad you came."

She kissed him back again. "I'm glad I came, too."

He kissed her mouth, gently at first, then more passionately as he tasted her and felt the compliance in her body as she leaned into him.

Within the intimate circle of his arms, she molded herself against his body and kissed him back.

When they finally broke the kiss, Archer felt more complete than he had ever felt before. He touched her hair, loving the feel of its soft thickness. "How are you?"

"Much better, thank you." She sounded breathless.

He became concerned. "Were you sick?"

"No. I'm just feeling better now," she said, allowing a small smile to peep out.

It warmed him all over. "Would you like a drink?" he asked, finally letting go of her long enough to shut the door and lead her into the living room.

Her big gray eyes darted all around, taking in everything. Wherever her gaze rested momentarily, he followed, seeing his own possessions through her eyes.

Still keeping his focus on Melody, he walked to a small teak cart and poured a glass of Chardonnay from the bottle chilling on ice. He walked back to her side and handed her the wine. "Check it out," he said, motioning with his own glass toward the photos that had just caught her attention. Then he watched as she sipped and moved around the room, studying each photograph, one at a time.

"They're beautiful," she murmured, her tone soft and reverent, as if she understood what the man behind the camera was trying to say.

"So are you."

She smiled, and her expression was so hesitant and shy he wanted to hold her again and let her know it was all right. Come to think of it, from the moment he'd stopped preparing for the evening and she walked in he'd wanted to hold her. For that reason alone, he forced himself not to.

When she was through making the rounds, he led her into the kitchen. It was all stainless steel and granite counters. He refused to think of how many shoots it had taken to pay for those damn counters, but only the best would do. He wanted what others would recognize as quality, and he got it.

"Hungry?"

"Yes," she said, sitting on the tall kitchen stool. "And I look forward to being served. What are we having?"

Archer pulled two dishes from the oven and one from the fridge. The dining table was already set and waiting for the entrée. "Mysteries from the Far East," he intoned.

She took a sniff. "Did you cook this?"

He grinned. "Of course."

Her easy laughter felt like a warm blanket. "Liar."

"How'd you know?"

"The cartons are in your trash can." She pointed to the corner.

He wasn't the least bit sorry. "Believe me, you'll like this a whole lot better than my cooking. Then we're going for a drive to see the New York I like. The one that tells me I'm on top of the world."

They ate their gourmet feast leisurely, talking about the past weekend, his work, her work, anything that popped up. He wanted to make love to her, but even more than that he simply wanted her here, in his home. Her conversation, her thoughts and her smile lit up a dark spot in his heart and he wanted to hang on to that lightness.

It really was odd. He'd never trusted the women in his life, yet, this total stranger had come along and he trusted her with thoughts and feelings he'd never voiced before, those little secrets he'd always held private. It was a wonder, and it was a shock to realize that he trusted her so much. It was all too new.

After dinner, Melody helped him clean up, telling him about Crystal's newest conquest, giggling over a joke another girlfriend had told her, telling him about a young man in her class who had more problems than the law allowed. In fact, the law had carted him out of class, taking him to the station for theft of the tape player he used to record Melody's lectures.

He loved listening to her. And she was like a spring bud, unfurling under the warmth of his attention.

When the few dishes were done, Archer took her arm and led her out the door, into the elevator and down to a cab stand outside his building.

"Where are we going?"

"To have dessert."

"Where?" she persisted.

"You'll see."

MELODY HAD HAD A LOT of dates, but this one was so different from any other that she wasn't sure what came next. But then, she'd already known that Archer was no run-of-the-mill date.

Their cab pulled up to the World Trade Center and Archer stepped out. With a disarming grin, he helped her from the car and they walked inside, toward the elevators.

A few minutes later they were at the top of the building seated in the restaurant overlooking the harbor. The Statue of Liberty was lit up in all its glory, completing a beautiful view that brought out the best of the Island.

The waitress, obviously a model wanna-be, showed them to their table, gave Archer an intimate wink and took their orders.

"Someone you know?" Melody asked sweetly,

biting her tongue to keep from sounding like a possessive shrew.

"I use her for catalogs off and on. She's the one who reserved the table for me."

"How sweet." Grudgingly, it was kind of the girl. And it showed that Archer cared enough to plan ahead for their time together.

"Don't get catty, Melody," Archer warned softly. "I was trying to do something nice. I thought you might enjoy it, too. That's all."

He'd read her but it was a little late. She'd already come to the same conclusion. She nodded. "Gotcha."

His brows rose. "That's it? Gotcha?"

"Yup."

"No complaints, recrimination, burial rights?"

"None."

He grinned. "Well, all right, then."

Dessert was a pie that was decadently filled, covered and drizzled in chocolate. They ordered coffees and shared one piece.

The waitress continued to hover, her gaze on Archer most of the time, with a few glances toward Melody. It was obvious she was wondering what Archer was doing with someone like her.

Beautiful women kept dropping by the table, ignoring Melody and drooling over Archer before drifting away. It reminded Melody of dining with her parents. There wasn't a restaurant in New York where her father wasn't recognized and approached. She was used to being ignored, unless someone could score points by acknowledging her. Apparently, it was no different with Archer.

Once or twice, though, Melody noticed him becoming impatient with the interruptions. But he never lost his cool and she was impressed by his ease. He had the polish of a much older man. He acted like the leader she was just realizing he was.

When they left, he waved to half a dozen more people. Apparently, this was a popular watering spot.

They took a cab back to Archer's place where they sat on the couch and drank coffee and talked—this time without interruptions. The stereo played classic rock and roll in the background. The city twinkled outside the windows.

Archer held her against him, spoon-style on the length of the couch cushion. Stroking her skin, he rested his head next to hers and looked at the sky, the lights of the city twinkling like a million stars.

"Archer?"

"Hmm?"

"Were most of those women models?"

He nuzzled her neck. "Some, but not all. The brunette is a corporate sponsor for one of the nonprofit catalogs I do. She pretends she's empty-headed, but she owns a classy newspaper in New England."

"I would never have known."

"She keeps it quiet. But I know."

"Does she know you know?"

Archer laughed. "I don't think so. But sooner

or later, she'll need my services, and I'll be in the front-row seat.''

A cold chill went down her spine at the thought. That had been the same problem she'd had with dates who knew who her father was. Halfway into the relationship, she'd find out they wanted a job, or a promotion, or the boss's daughter because they thought the money would keep on flowing. She wouldn't put herself in that position again.

''Isn't that sneaky?''

''No. It's just quiet information. I found out when I was doing her catalog. Everyone in her office knows who she is—it's no secret. It's just that we never talked about it.''

''Were you…are you…?''

''Melody,'' he began.

But she was quicker. ''Never mind. I don't want to know.''

''Good, because it has nothing to do with us one way or another.''

''You're right.''

Silence filtered through the room. The compact disc ended and another started up. A slow, sultry tune with an alto sax began its magic.

''But if I did date any of them for longer than a month,'' Archer whispered, ''I don't remember.''

''Oh, that's great,'' she stated dryly. ''I'm dating a man without a memory.'' She gave his arm a light pinch.

''Aren't you the lucky one,'' he said in her ear. ''Since I don't remember whether or not I kissed you, I'll have to do it again.''

"Oh, poor baby," she crooned, and felt the tension leaving her. "I'll prompt you for the rest of the evening."

He turned her in his arms then, until he had access to her mouth.... And later, when Archer pulled her up and led her to his loft bedroom, she followed willingly because she wanted him as much as he wanted her.

But once they got there Melody took the lead and made love to Archer for the first time. Being in control was the most wonderful, scary feeling she'd ever experienced.

8

ARCHER LEANED THROUGH the back window of the cab so he could kiss Melody before she left. She had to be home in the morning to meet her parents who were coming for their usual mid-week breakfast. Only God, death or a business trip could keep them away, which was her reason for not staying the night with him.

But Archer wasn't letting her go until he made sure Melody understood this wasn't their last date. He had plans for her. Lots of them. "I have to leave tomorrow for a shoot in the Caribbean, but I want to see you when I get back."

"How long will you be gone?" she asked in a sad voice.

He silently cursed the contract that was taking him away from the woman—the first and only woman—he loved. "Four days, maybe five. Tops."

Her hand covered his. "I'll miss you," she said softly, and he wanted to pull her from the cab and drown in those big gray eyes of hers.

He gave her one quick, hard kiss. "Something else is brewing as far as work goes, and if it plays out, I may not be traveling as much. But don't forget me while I'm gone, okay? I'll call."

She nodded. Archer leaned down and placed one more kiss on her mouth, then thumped the driver's door twice. "Okay," he called.

He didn't bother watching her go. He didn't want to see her leave.

The driver sped off before she could roll up the window. Her gaze followed Archer as he disappeared inside the building. She clutched her small birthday bag close. Inside was his gift to remember him by.

Then she sat back and hugged her love to herself. While he might not love her, he liked her far more than he knew. She was sure. She was almost positive.

Well, maybe.

Up bubbled her joy again and she wanted to shout out her feelings to everyone on the street.

The cab passed the Waldorf-Astoria and she laughed. Her relationship with Archer had started there. Amazing. What a wonderful, extravagant, fabulous hotel!

She had Crystal to thank for all of this. Crystal had chosen so well, knowing Melody's type far better than Melody obviously did. It had worked! She owed it all to Crystal.

That reminded her that Crystal had teased her into springing for a Caribbean trip. Wouldn't it be fun if they went where Archer was? He could get away from the job—

No. She knew better than that. And it wasn't fair to put him in that position. Besides, she wasn't sure if his feelings were strong enough to stand the obvious comparison of sleek and photogenic models versus full-figured and kinda cute Melody. She wasn't brave enough to test that theory.

She'd wait here until he returned.

Even that gave her a warm feeling. She was waiting for her man to return from work. Yes. That sounded good. Nice. Domestic. Womanly.

That night, curled in bed with a pillow in place of Archer, she dreamed of being domestic. Of being a wife and mom. She had so much love to give and, finally, just the man to give it to. If Archer gave her a chance, she could make him happy—she knew it.

HER PARENTS ARRIVED AT the apartment, exactly on time, as usual. They held newspapers, several bakery boxes and three containers that Melody knew contained fresh-made omelets from their favorite restaurant. Also, as usual. Melody always supplied freshly brewed coffee, her father's favorite brand that was flown in from Seattle on a weekly basis.

"Hello, dear." Her father bent over to kiss Melody on the cheek while carefully holding his expensive gray suit coat and tie to his stomach, as if she were still a child covered in dirt and grime.

He was an impeccably dressed, handsome man, with his square face and strong jaw, and gray eyes so very much like her own. But he seldom smiled and his brow had permanent frown lines that gave him a stern look. As far as Melody could remember, he'd never been a jovial man, nor worn a sense of humor for longer than it took for someone to tell him a joke and for him to laugh.

Emma Chase kissed Melody's other cheek. Her dark hair was cropped short and hugged her perfectly shaped head. Her makeup was impeccable and classically stated. She was dressed in an electric-blue Armani suit. Unlike Melody, her mother looked beautiful in designer clothes. She could have passed for a model.

"Hello, Dad. Mother." She shut the door and led the way into the kitchen where the table was already set for breakfast, right down to the cloth napkins. Her father hated using paper when it wasn't necessary—he had strong feelings around environmental issues. Several of his publishing companies used only recycled paper.

While her father made the toast, her mother tested the coffee and pronounced it drinkable. Melody transferred the omelets to her good china—a gift from her parents for her birthday last year. The only time she ever used it was when they came over. She didn't even like the design.

Melody knew she should have opened her mouth and protested a present she didn't want or need, but she'd tried declining favors before and all it did was create conflict without compromise. She finally decided that her parents were...well, her parents. They took personal satisfaction in giving her what *they* thought she needed. She could put up with that sort of stuff as long as they allowed her to live her own life.

"So tell me all about the Heart Books bachelor

auction," her mother said conversationally, as if they'd never argued over this very subject. "I should have gone with you."

"I thought you didn't approve of 'that sort of display,'" Melody quoted.

Her mother studiously buttered some toast and set it just so on the side of her father's plate. "Well, yes, but I would have gone for your sake."

"Thanks. Crystal went with me."

Her mother scrunched up her face, but didn't say anything. Nothing Emma Chase had said before had hindered the friendship, nor had the dossier her people had compiled on Crystal.

In fact, in a rare display of temper, Melody had thrown the papers into the fireplace and threatened never to see her parents again unless they stopped monitoring her life and the life of her friends. They had reluctantly agreed, but it didn't stop them doing it to the men they kept parading before her.

Her mother interrupted her thoughts. "And what was the auction like, darling?"

"I told you already. I bid on the fashion photographer, Archer, and won a weekend in the Poconos and a photo shoot."

Her father unfolded one of five newspapers he'd brought with him. "Which you paid for and haven't received."

"The money went for a good cause, Dad."

Her father grunted and glanced up. "That's good."

Her mother looked relieved and went back to her inquisition. "Did you enjoy yourself, dear?"

"The Poconos is a lovely spot. And I enjoyed watching the photographer and the reporter work." She smiled blandly.

"How exciting. Was he nice?"

"He?" An image of Archer naked as he stepped into the spa popped into her head. She gave a cough to cover the gasp caught in her throat. "Preoccupied with his career. He took pictures everywhere we went."

"You didn't meet anyone else while you were there?"

She was supposed to be looking under every leaf and blade of grass. "Not a soul."

"So sorry, dear," her mother said, patting her hand. "At least the money went for a good cause. Your father's right. Everyone needs to read more."

Her father looked around the edge of the paper and over the rim of his bifocals. They were a recent addition to his wardrobe and he only wore them in private. Most of his office staff put up with his squinting when he was in public. "Your mother has an idea we think you'll like."

Melody's heart gave a squeeze. Not another blind date, please…

"There's a young man working for the new magazine I'm planning to acquire. We're still in negotiations. His name is Stan. Divorced."

Her mother brushed that away with a wave of her hand. "Yes, but his wife left him for another man. Can you imagine? I don't understand how people can just walk away from the sanctity of marriage."

"Maybe he ignored her, or cheated on her, or wasn't there for her," Melody suggested.

Her mother shook her head. "Marriage is sacred, and shouldn't be discarded easily."

Her mother was adamant on this point. Always. Melody knew she wasn't going to win this one, but she'd go down trying. "But he did. For whatever reason, he divorced."

"I know, but I think he's learned his lesson." Her mother paused to take a bite of her omelet, then frowned and asked, "By the way, whatever happened to that nice young man you dated for a couple of months last year?"

"Brock?" Melody gave a sigh. "Mother, he was only borderline nice and a lot preoccupied. He was a workaholic. He broke half the dates we made."

"In my day 'workaholic' wasn't an ugly word," her father said from behind the paper.

"In your day, Dad, it was a badge of honor, and noble excuse for ignoring whatever else was going on in life."

His paper rattled, but it was her mother who spoke up. "That's unfair, Melody. Your father works hard for us. You and I as well as twelve-thousand employees reap the rewards of his labor, as will your children."

"Sorry," Melody said, and she meant it. It wasn't her father's fault—this was a very old argument that wasn't going to be solved in *her* generation.

"Besides, what's wrong with being a workaholic? Brock still seemed nice."

"Mother, he sent me a birthday card with his business card in it instead of a signature!"

"Then you could always send it to someone else again," said her <u>mother</u> the optimist.

"Great," Melody said dryly. "I now have my mother's permission to send a love poem to a man, but without an envelope that fits." Despite herself, she giggled.

The paper rattled.

Her mother smiled.

All was right with the Chase family world.

They ate in peace, talking off and on about what was going on in the family.

Her parents left earlier than usual. Her father had a board meeting and her mother was going straight to a charity luncheon. Melody picked up the textbook she was reviewing for her class. But her thoughts were elsewhere...in the Caribbean.

MELODY COUNTED THE days until Archer came home. He called every evening from his hotel, but they could never talk long enough.

Less than a week later, Archer called from his studio. "Hello, sexy. How are you, and when can I see you again?"

She smiled so broadly, she was sure he could see it over the phone. "Hello, yourself and I'm fine. How about tonight at my place?"

"What time?"

"Seven?"

"Great. Are you feeding me or should I stop somewhere on the way?"

"I'll feed you, I'll feed you," she laughed. "And I'll actually do the cooking myself."

"Don't go out of your way, now," he teased. "I can always buy a hot dog and a pretzel."

"Just be on time, Mr. Archer, or you'll starve to death because I have plans for your body and you need your energy."

His laughter rang in her ears as she hung up and her heart did somersaults. She ran to the kitchen, made a list of what she'd need for dinner, then headed for the grocery store. An hour later, she was back and cooking.

By seven o'clock she was ready. The meal was cooked to perfection and the table was set with fine linen and candles. She sipped on her glass of wine, bathed and dressed with care, and anticipated Archer's arrival.

When he reached her door, looking tall, handsome and extremely sexy, food was the last thing on her mind. But suddenly she felt shy and awkward.

Thank goodness, he didn't.

Just as he had the last time they'd met, he circled her waist with his arms and pulled her as close as he could to his own rock-hard body. "Hello, sweet thing."

"Hello, you handsome hunk." She'd wanted to say "*my* hunk" and that came through in her tone. Her voice was a whisper that he swallowed up in his kiss.

She didn't mind at all.

They shed their clothing and made love on the

living room floor in front of the fireplace that held spring flowers.

They didn't eat until midnight, but she'd planned for that possibility when she'd chosen the menu. They ate sitting on the floor, with a lit six-scone candelabra on the hearth to light the room.

Archer leaned against the couch, mouthwateringly naked, one leg stretched in front of him and the other crooked as he peeled and fed her slices of orange for dessert.

Melody wasn't quite that brave. She wasn't willing to let him see her in all her naked, imperfect glory all evening long.

Instead, she wore his shirt.

He fed her another bite. "Did I already mention what a nice apartment you have?"

"Yes, and thank you." She opened her mouth; he popped a piece of fruit in.

He looked around the well-appointed apartment. "Was this part of your inheritance?"

She was reluctant to discuss her family situation, but knew she had to keep their relationship honest. "My aunt left it to me when she died." She didn't mention that her father had bought it for his sister to begin with.

"Nice relatives." He looked at the tasteful furniture, the silky Bokara rug on which they sat. "And wealthy. I'd guess." His gaze touched on the paintings on the wall. Some were collectable and signed lithographs, some were originals, including two Dalis, if he wasn't mistaken.

"Very nice. And yes, the family is wealthy and

I'm the only child. And they drive me crazy."
That was an honest answer. "What about your
parents?"

"My dad was a bouncer in Atlantic City who
disappeared before I was born. My mom worked
as a change maker in the casinos and now han-
dles a blackjack table. No siblings." He spoke
with so little emotion that she knew there was a
lot of hurt buried in those words. She recognized
the symptoms.

"It had to be interesting growing up in such an
active area. All the gambling and the Miss America Pageant. I've only been on the Boardwalk
once, but I liked it."

"I didn't think it was wonderful at all," he
said, studiously examining the orange while
peeling off another section and placing it in front
of her lips.

"How did you learn photography?" she asked
before taking it from him.

"I was always interested in cameras. For a
while I learned from an old friend of the family,
on the Boardwalk. When I'd learned enough, I
came to the big city."

She was sure that story carried about as much
truth as hers did. She just wasn't certain where
the omissions were buried.

"Do you like what you do?"

"I love it." He was back on firm ground. She
was back to believing every word he spoke. "As
a matter of fact, I haven't had much of a private
life because of what I do. My career has always
come first. It's only been, uh, recently, that I re-

alized that I might be missing something." He grinned, giving her a knowing look that made her heart beat faster.

She felt her cheeks grow hot. "But with so many beautiful women around you all the time—"

He laughed out loud before she could finish. "Those aren't women. Those are walking, talking mannequins. They are so career oriented they don't want anyone in their lives, unless it's a millionaire with one foot in the grave. Besides, they're emaciated, nothing but skin and bones."

"Every man's dream."

He looked at her as if she were crazy. "Not this guy's dream. You're far sexier than any of them, any day of the week."

She was sure he was lying, but she loved him for it. His opinions soothed her ego and made her feel even better about herself than she did already. "Really?"

He leaned over and pulled her toward him, his grin was absolutely wicked. He ran his hand through her hair, holding her still as he sipped at her neck. "Really. Now, you—you're a different story. I can trust you. If you say something, it's so. That's rare, Melody Chase. Very rare. An honest woman. Just exactly what the doctor ordered."

"Everybody lies now and then," Melody said, suddenly feeling uncomfortable. This was the time to tell him who her father was. But then she told herself that another time, one not so romantic, would present itself. Then she'd tell him.

"Hey, woman, shut up and make love with me. I'm dying for the taste of you."

Shoving aside her doubts, she did exactly as he demanded. And she tasted of him as well....

It was three o'clock in the morning before Archer called for a cab and Melody said goodbye to him at the door. It was five o'clock before she closed her eyes.

But she never stopped dreaming....

ARCHER CALLED HER every afternoon. She called him in the evening after class. In between times, they met at her place or his.

Melody finally admitted to herself just how much she was in love with Archer, but she was afraid to tell him. Afraid to speak the words aloud, even to Crystal.

And she was equally afraid to tell him the truth about her money and her father. He might decide they were from different worlds. He wouldn't realize that her wealthy upbringing wasn't too much different than his upbringing in poverty; they'd both been emotionally starved.

One evening after class, she met Crystal at their favorite bar. They found a table scrunched against the front glass, ordered two glasses of wine, and Melody talked.

"Okay, so you love him," Crystal said after Melody finally admitted the fact. "Now what?"

"I don't know," she answered. "I'm so darn confused. I think he loves me, too, but he's never said a word about love or commitment or marriage. He hasn't even mentioned whether or not he wants children."

"But he knows you want children, doesn't he?"

"Yes, he's known that from the beginning. But he's never said a word about wanting children of his own."

"So-o-o," Crystal said, drawing out the word. "Ask him."

"Just come right out with it?"

Crystal nodded, her blond hair glinting and catching half a dozen male gazes. She didn't seem to notice.

"I can't do that."

"Why not? Is he hard of hearing?"

"No, but," Melody stopped. "What would I say?"

"You'd say, 'we've talked about what I want for my future, but I've never asked you about yours.' Then wait and see what he has to say."

Melody eyed her friend. "You're good."

Crystal bowed her head in acknowledgment. "Thank you so much for recognizing my talent."

Melody turned solemn. "Crystal, what happens if Archer dodges the real question?"

"Then you love someone who will probably make you terribly unhappy and you need to stay away from him until finally you don't love him anymore."

"Great." Melody hid a sniffle. "I'm seeing him tomorrow night. After that, I'll be able to assess my options."

"Good." Crystal leaned forward, a smile on

her full lips. Looking as if she was sharing a secret, she said, "When we leave here, I want you to notice the guy standing in the gray trench coat at the end of the bar. He's carrying on a conversation with a guy in a red warm-up suit. He has a beautiful smile, twinkling blue eyes and a receding hairline, and I want to have his babies."

Melody glanced toward the bar.

"Don't look now!" Crystal said.

"Why not? He isn't paying attention." At that moment he turned his head and stared straight at her. Melody smiled. He nodded and turned back to his friend. They both laughed about something. Melody hoped she wasn't the brunt of a joke. "Besides, you can't tell whether he's got blue eyes from here or not."

Crystal looked down at her manicure. "It's *my* fantasy. I'll give him whatever color eyes I want."

She was right. Everyone was entitled to their fantasies. Heaven only knew, Melody was going to do her best to fantasize herself into dreamland tonight.

Imagine Archer wanting to marry her so she could have his babies!

"ARCHER?"

He was playing with lighting umbrellas accenting a gray, velvet-covered table holding several sets of spike-heeled shoes. "Hmm?"

Melody was perched on a wooden stool next to the tripod camera and watching him work. His eye for detail was amazing. She'd observed him for the past hour and wondered at his patience and talent.

But now she wanted his attention. She wiggled a little on the wooden seat and tried to sound casual, as she broached her subject. "You know, Archer, we've talked about what I want in my future, but I've never asked you about yours," she ventured. "What is it you want to happen in your personal life?"

"I want to get these shoes on film so I can stop for the night and make love to you in the corner of the studio on that pile of furs over there." Without looking "over there," he motioned in that general direction. Then he carefully tipped one shoe in a slightly different direction.

"Then what?" she prompted.

"Then I want to order dinner from the restaurant across the street and eat it with you on my lap. And tonight, I want you to promise to spend the night."

Even though he said it in an absentminded kind of voice, the thought made her warm all over. "I hadn't planned on it."

"Don't you think this is the night?" He grinned over his shoulder. "I mean, think of it. We won't have to worry about waiting for cabs on the early morning streets of New York."

He was right there, she thought, but that wasn't what she'd wanted to hear. What she wanted was Archer's full attention and for him to give her a declaration of love. She wanted him to voice the words she didn't dare say to him.

She wanted the happy ending, only she wanted it to be the beginning.

"Archer," she began, disappointed. If Crystal was right, Archer was neatly fitting into her description of the "artful dodger." Damn. He was hunkering down in front of the display, his faded jeans lovingly molding to his buns, a well-worn T-shirt fitting him like faded blue paint. But she was momentarily sidetracked.

He looked over his shoulder, his gaze catching hers and growing so intense she could feel the heat of it. "And, by the way, I want a personal life, too. I also want a family. And I want someone who understands my needs and wants and who'll share their private and personal thoughts with me."

The breath eased from her lungs. Her grin began slowly, spreading over her face like a beacon. "That's nice to hear," she finally said.

He smiled. "I thought you might like to hear it. Especially since I meant to tell you before this, but the opportunity never came up."

As happy as she'd been with Archer in her life until now, she'd never felt this happy ever before.

She was one step closer to telling him she was in love with him. But maybe, just maybe, he'd say it before she did.

The phone on the wall rang, and Archer cursed under his breath. "Would you get that for me, honey? I'm expecting a call from a magazine mogul."

Melody scooted off the stool and went to the phone. "At this time of night?"

He laughed. "Haven't you noticed yet that there are no times a photographer doesn't work?"

She didn't answer. "Archer Photography," she said.

"Who is this?" a female voice demanded.

"Melody Chase. Who is this?"

"I want to speak to Archer." So much for manners.

"May I tell him who's calling?"

"None of your damn business."

Melody walked back to Archer's side. "A jealous rival," she whispered, hoping she was kidding. But the woman on the phone was upset about something.

Archer took the phone. His face turned to stone. "This isn't a conversation I need to have with you. It's over, remember?"

The woman spoke.

"Don't even bother. I don't want to see or hear from you again until you can behave yourself and act like a friend. Not, I repeat, not a girlfriend. Never again, Sondra."

With exact precision, he took the phone away from his ear, and while Melody could still hear Sondra talking, he severed the connection.

She waited for him to say something. Instead, he hung his head and stared at the floor, deep in thought.

After the silence stretched out for several

minutes, Melody couldn't stand it anymore. "Archer? Are you all right?"

He looked up at her blankly, slowly returning to the room from whatever thoughts had engulfed him. A small, sad smile tilted the corners of his mouth. "You're very special. Did I mention that before?"

"No, but thank you." She waited another moment.

"Are you ever jealous of the women I work with?" he asked softly.

She didn't know where this was leading, but she knew she had to answer from her heart. "Occasionally, I am. But I know if you wanted to have a fling with a model, there is nothing I could do to stop you. I also know that if anything was happening between you and one of them, you wouldn't continue with me. You'd be busy. All I can do is either trust you or leave."

"You're right. And thanks for the vote of confidence." He placed the phone on the small table and walked over to her. "I can't tell you how much I value your trust and your honesty, Melody. I need that in my life more than I've ever needed anything else. And you give me that like a big gift wrapped up with a bow." He kissed her mouth lightly. "What a wonderful woman you are," he said softly as he took her in his arms and held her close to his heart. "I'm so glad I found you." He kissed her then, with a deep tenderness that couldn't be sourced from less than love.

She blushed with pleasure. Apparently that

phone call had been from an old girlfriend who felt spurned.

She felt triumphant. But, in the back of her mind, her conscience gave a twinge. She hadn't told him about her very wealthy parents and what they owned. She would, just as soon as the right moment arose. But not now. Certainly, not now...

It was a romantic night to remember. Archer fed her, laughed with her and made love to her as if he'd just found the secret of the universe. And when he placed her in a cab the next morning, her skin was still tingling from his touch.

When her cell phone rang, she was almost reluctant to answer and let the world intrude upon her dreams. But she did.

"Hello, Mother," she said and her mother began talking without preamble. She had set up the *dreaded date* with Stan for the following night at her parents' home for dinner. Stan probably thought she was a real dog if her parents had to get her a date, but the poor guy was still willing to do what the boss wanted. As far as she was concerned, that said a lot about his personality.

She put her mother off by telling her she had two dates this week, and that they would talk tomorrow. Her mother was elated. Melody was dating, and that was enough for the time being.

When she slipped the phone back in her purse, she knew she had to tell her mother to back off, once and for all.

She did not want a man like her father for a marriage partner—consumed and introverted and controlling. That might be her mother's ideal, but the very thought of being with someone like that for the rest of her life frightened Melody more than words could say.

When her parents showed up at breakfast next week, she'd have a heart-to-heart talk to them. She just hoped they'd listen.

9

From the moment her parents phoned early Wednesday morning to say they'd be late for breakfast, Melody felt a sense of dread. There was no reason for it. Nothing bad had happened—just some papers her father had to sign for his latest merger to go through.

Two minutes later, her phone rang again, but this time it was Archer and her heart did a flip in excitement.

"I've been offered that plum job I was hinting at, darlin'," he said, unable to keep the excitement out of his voice. "Four different fashion magazines have just merged and they want me to choreograph all the photo shoots. It's a hefty salary, and I'll still be able to run my own business on the side, if I want to."

"That's fantastic!"

"I'm happy." She could tell that was an understatement. His voice barely contained his enjoyment at the very thought.

"Which magazines?" she asked, fearful that they might belong to her father.

He named them and they were all well respected and, thankfully, not among her father's holdings. Archer's excitement was catching; she knew from their talks just how much this meant to him. It was the next rung on the ladder, and an opportunity to learn new skills. "That's wonderful! When did this happen?"

"The offer was formally made this morning." He sounded on top of the world. "I'm taking it to my attorney right now. But if the deal is as good as I think it is, I'm signing. No more traveling around the country and taking a red-eye back in time to work again the next morning. I'll have time for us. For what we want."

"And what do we want?" she asked, gripping the phone.

"You know and I know." Archer's voice told her he wasn't buying her innocence. "We'll discuss it next time."

When Archer hung up, Melody should have felt wonderful, and a part of her did.

Home. Archer would be home more often. How wonderful! But she still had the niggling feeling that something was going to go wrong.

When the phone rang again, it was an old boyfriend she hadn't heard from in three years. He was just touching base with her, he said, and wanted to know if they could have lunch sometime. Not wanting to beat around the bush, Melody explained that she was involved with someone else and would rather not. But he was undaunted. He gave her his new phone number just in case she changed her mind. Melody didn't have the heart to tell him she had it on Caller ID already and would never call him—not even if a bomb dropped tomorrow and they were the only two people left on earth.

She had two more phone calls from old boyfriends, but she saw the name and number and didn't bother to answer either of them.

But it made her wonder what was going on. Was there something in the water? Why today? She hadn't heard from any of the three of them in over a year. Now, all at once, they decide to call before ten o'clock in the morning?

It was the sixth phone call that gave her the explanation—and a reason for her feeling of dread.

"Have you seen the latest copy of *Personal*?" Crystal didn't waste time on pleasantries, she went directly to the heart of the conversation regarding a weekly celebrity tabloid.

"No," Melody said dryly. "I stopped all subscriptions to gossip rags delivered to my door."

"I wouldn't miss an issue," Crystal stated. "But that's beside the point. This edition is special. There's an article about you and lover boy in there, and you're not going to like it."

There it was—the thing she'd woken up dreading this morning.

"Read it to me," she said, dead calm in her voice. But her hands shook.

The article stated that Archer had arranged to have Melody Chase, daughter of Ian Chase, magazine mogul, bid for him at a charity auction so Archer could wrangle his way into her family and become a part of the wealthy magazine dynasty. It even said that his ploy had worked, for he'd been offered a multimagazine contract as

head of photography. So, Melody Chase, poor little rich girl, was being pursued for nefarious reasons by the big, bad, social-climbing photographer. And rumors abounded that this wasn't the
only time Daddy had bought a man for her....

"Dear sweet heaven," Melody breathed when
Crystal finished reading. "My parents don't even
know Archer is in my life. And Archer doesn't
know who my dad is."

"You didn't tell him? Them?" Crystal's voice
rose in disbelief.

"I never got around to it," she hedged.

But Crystal was relentless. "Why in the name
of Zeus didn't you?"

She gave in with a resigned sigh. "Because I
didn't want Archer to run away. He's so darn in-
dependent, he'd never have a thing to do with
me if he knew. Besides, that's nothing new. I
don't tell anyone about my family. You know as
well as I do that when most men find out, they either want a closer relationship instantly, or run
like heck. I wanted Archer in my life for me, not
for any other of a million dollar reasons." She
suddenly realized why all those wimps of old
boyfriends had been calling. She never told anyone about her family unless they were close to
her, and boyfriends didn't count as close until
they proposed and she accepted....

"Poor little rich girl," Crystal said in a dry
voice.

But Melody didn't hear. She was too busy with
her own thoughts. "I did this all wrong," she
said, more to herself than to Crystal. Deceptions.

Dishonesty. Archer's big buggaboo. She'd meant to tell him about her dad, but the time was never right. It never would be, she realized.

"Call him quick and let him know before someone else tells him."

"Good advice. Thanks, friend. Talk to you later," she said, then hung up the phone.

After quickly brushing her teeth and running a comb through her hair, Melody began making coffee for her parents. While setting the table, she tried calling Archer.

He didn't answer. Instead, his machine picked up so she left a message.

A little later she tried again, but didn't even get his answering machine this time.

She paged him.

He didn't return the call.

By the time her parents arrived, she was a bundle of nerves. Her dad carried the gossip magazine conspicuously under his arm. His face resembled a thundercloud and she knew from experience he wanted to take her to task for a serious offense.

"Who is this Archer guy and why do you have anything to do with him?" her father asked suspiciously. "I thought we agreed that you'd tell me about anyone you dated from my company."

The glint in her eye should have warned him he was in for battle. "I bought a weekend with him in the Poconos at a charity auction, just like the magazine said, Daddy."

He ignored her explanation. "You promised you'd let me know so I could be prepared for things like this. You've let me down, pumpkin. I expected you to honor your promise."

She took a deep breath and began again. "Until this morning, he wasn't working for one of your magazines. Archer has his own company. He still doesn't know about you or what you do."

Her father continued to frown. "I don't like it. Everyone's assuming I just signed those contracts this morning to give him a job because he dates you, young lady."

Her heart squeezed with that ol' demon, dread. "He's not going to be too happy about it, either."

"I don't know why not," her mother stated loyally. "Your father is one of the most influential men in the country. Your *friend* is just a photographer. He should be flattered. He got good publicity, while your father looked as if he were bowing to the whims of his daughter."

"Which he's never been accused of before in his life," Melody added. But she knew it would be wasted on her parents. They didn't quite see things the way she did.

"You might find it funny to look down your nose at what your father's accomplished, but no one seems to mind when they're standing in line for the money, do they? Including this Archer, who was in the auction you paid for by your father's labor."

"Labor?" Melody knew how much was in her trust fund, to say nothing of savings, her unlimited bank cards or her bank account. Her inheritance.

"Mother, I…" she began, knowing full well she was going to lose. "I'm sorry."

The doorbell pealed through the silence in the room. No one had called through the security desk, so it had to be a neighbor. She was relieved for the interruption.

But when she opened the door, it was to behold the most frustrated male she'd ever seen. And, darn if she wasn't the one he was frustrated with. His thick, blond hair looked as if he'd run his hands through it a hundred times. His stance was belligerent; he was ready to erupt at any moment. His brown eyes shot fire that could have lit her fireplace from across the room.

The magazine was rolled and clutched in his fist. "Tell me this is a lie."

"Archer, I—"

"Tell me," he demanded in a low voice that filled her with the dread she'd been feeling all morning. She should have known it would all blow up in her face. She'd heard warning bells every time an opening had come to tell the truth and she hadn't taken it.

"Tell me you haven't been dishonest with me all this time."

This scene would be forever etched in her mind. Archer standing in the closed doorway. Her father, barely visible, standing in the kitchen doorway. Her caught in between the two, knowing the anger of both.

"You knew how I felt about lies in a relationship. You knew I was proud of my business. And you never let me know about your own background. You never said a word, Melody. That was a *dirty rotten thing to do!*"

"I didn't know my father was buying the company, Archer," she said. But his frosty brown eyes told her he didn't believe her.

With deliberate steps, he strode past her and stood in the middle of the living room. He stared at the carpet as if he were seeing something there.

"Archer?" she asked, slowly following him. "What is it?"

When he looked at her, the anger had been frozen—he had cut her out of his life. She knew it as surely as she knew her sin. "I just wanted to check out the site where you seduced me before emotionally trussing me up like a Christmas turkey to make it look publicly like I sold my integrity."

"I didn't do it to hurt you. I did it to protect myself." Her words fell on deaf ears.

His heart was hard as granite. "I need to burn that impression deep in my brain so I know never to get in bed with a lying woman like you, again."

It was a slap in the face and she felt so very hurt. But slowly, her own anger was building. "I admit, it was my fault I didn't tell you who my father was, but that's all I'm guilty of, Archer." She took a step toward him, but he backed a step away. It was her turn to feel frustrated and angry. How many times did she need to say it before he believed her?

"Please, don't screw me around any more than you already have," he said in disgust. "If I ever live this down, it'll be a miracle."

"But, Archer…"

He didn't want to hear an explanation. He was too angry. "You could have played around in my personal life and I would have recovered. But you didn't. You went straight for the jugular, Melody. You made a fool of me in my own business. The one place I don't mess around. You see, I don't have Daddy's dollars behind me to clean up any mess I make. I've just got me, the poor kid from Atlantic City who worked his butt off to get where I am."

"And if I could change things, I would." Her voice was low, but filled with meaning.

It was as if she never spoke. "But you knew that, and still you continued to lie about your connections. Right up till this morning."

"Is this the young man I'm supposed to hire because you think he's so talented?" Her father's booming voice broke in as he stepped away from the kitchen door.

Melody felt her cheeks redden. "Uh, Daddy, this is Archer of Archer Photography."

Archer's gaze filled with anger. "Don't bother with the introduction. He wouldn't acknowledge me at all if I wasn't standing in the center of his daughter's apartment." He raised a brow. "Or is this Daddy's, too?"

Her father stood straight and tall, looking

down his aristocratic nose. "As far as you're concerned, young man, it may as well be. And you obviously have my credentials. All I know about you is that you're a fashion photographer. Most are a dime a dozen."

Archer faced him, hands on his lean hips. It could have been a showdown between two gunfighters. Pride was what was going to pull the trigger. "Oh, well, that says it all, doesn't it?" Archer's voice was filled with sarcasm. "Except that I'm not one of the dozen. I'm better than good. I'm *damn* good. But you'll never know. You might buy and sell magazines, but I'd bet you don't have a clue how to put one together."

Melody watched the two men, suddenly in silent awe of all they might have in common. She'd never realized it before. How could she have been so dense? Both men were power hungry. They loved the fight and were sore losers. And they were both spoiling for a fight; either with her or with each other—they didn't care as long as they were in the heat of battle.

Two warrior kings of their domain, and neither willing to give. Pride was the chasm.

Her mother came to the kitchen door and watched the circus with a coffee cup in her hand. She could just as well have been in her penthouse on the patio watching sunrise over the skyline. It suddenly dawned on Melody that her mother had seen her father in this mode more often than Melody ever had. And she knew the outcome. It was written on her calm face. The whole thing was nature's way, survival of the fittest.

"I don't have to have know-how, young man. I find people who do. That's my area of expertise. Just like I'd hire you to do your job if you had an ounce of brains. But, I don't like being wrong, and from the looks of it, that's what I'd be. If you don't have the good sense to see the quality in my daughter, you certainly can't see anything else, either."

"Your daughter set me up to look like a fool. She knew that my career came first, no matter what. And that I make it on my own or not at all." He turned his head to glare at Melody. "But she didn't give a damn about any of that when she spoke to Sondra. She just spilled her guts at my expense."

"Sondra?" Melody felt confused. "Who's Sondra?"

"The journalist who wrote this piece of trash," her father answered without looking at her. "My people tell me she's worked at the magazine for the past two years." His gaze pierced through Archer. "And I use the term *journalist* loosely. But you know her, don't you?" He waited for an answer. None came. "And just for the record, my daughter has never sought out the press nor talked to them about her life. Never." He paused for emphasis. "But, Mr. Archer, it seems *you* know the woman on a first-name basis." His gaze pierced the younger man's. "How is that?"

"I know her." Archer's gaze was defiant. "I know her well enough to know that she wouldn't write this article without being sure of her sources."

"You also claim you don't know my daughter's morals, and yet, by your own admission, you went to bed with her."

The older man's pride and stiffness pierced Melody's heart. Although she wasn't ashamed, she wished her father hadn't heard all that.

Archer shrugged. "We all make mistakes."

The pain his words brought her was immeasurable. It pierced her heart and soul.

"It doesn't say much for your sense of decency, does it?" His wife moved forward to protectively circle his waist, but he didn't seem to notice. "Let's see if I get this right. You go to bed with a woman you don't know well enough to trust. And you are also intimate with a woman who calls herself a journalist, but is barely on the border of gossip columnist at a magazine that caters to prurient life-styles of the rich and decadent." Her father raised his thick brows. "And you've chosen to believe one of them on that basis." He gave a short bark of laughter. "Amazing how screwed up your sense of intuition is. I hope my attorneys were smart enough to provide an out clause in your contract."

"My business sense got me this far."

"No telling how far you could have gotten if you'd had good intuition to go along with it."

Archer and the older man stood head to head, glaring at each other. Melody watched in wonder at the silent challenge. What was this all about? Archer had made up his mind. And so had her father.

And now, so had Melody.

As far as she was concerned it was over. She walked to the door and opened it. "Thank you for coming and squaring away matters, Archer. I'm sorry for any misunderstanding I caused you. I'd like you to leave now." Her voice was low, but everyone heard the quiver—and the resolution.

Archer stared at her father for one more long moment. Then, with a nod toward her mother, he turned and walked out the door. He didn't give a backward glance. He didn't say a word, not even goodbye.

The only sound Melody heard was her heart breaking into tiny pieces.

She turned and closed the door behind her, wishing she was alone so she could collapse on the couch in a bucket of tears. But that wasn't to be.

Her father stood ramrod straight, staring at the same spot on the floor that Archer had walked to earlier. She knew what he was thinking and her skin pricked with guilt. Oh, not the guilt of making love with Archer. Never that. She loved him and if those were the only memories of him that she had to cherish, she was luckier than most.

But having her father embarrassed was... was... She was still searching for the word when her father turned and walked out the door to the hallway.

"Daddy?" she called, but he was gone, shutting the door behind him.

Her mother gave her a quick hug. "Give him time, honey. Until this minute, I don't think it ever dawned on him that his little girl had grown up."

Melody felt so humiliated. But it was not the end of the world. "He must have known dates occasionally lead to intimacy."

Her mother smiled a little, but it was as sad as a tear. "Never dawned on him, darling. Not once." She turned and headed out the door to follow her husband. "I'm guilty, too, honey. I didn't think much about it, either. But I was more prepared."

"Mom," she called, tears blurring her vision. One tear escaped to land quietly on her blouse.

Her mother glanced a kiss off her cheek. "I'll talk to you later, dear. I must get to your father."

She quickly walked out of the apartment, leaving Melody alone with her own private emotional mess.

As usual.

Melody shut the front door with a satisfying slam. All her life her parents had been able to push her buttons. Today, she allowed someone else to push them, too. Archer had no right to jump to those conclusions. He also had no right to spar with her father, but he seemed to be enjoying it.

Another tear dropped. She turned and stared into space.

No matter what happened, she didn't want a marriage like the one her parents had. She never wanted to feel like a second-class citizen just because she was a woman. She didn't want to spend the rest of her life taking care of a man instead of taking care of a child. Never. She'd rather be single and lonely the rest of her life than get caught in a marriage where her career wasn't as important as her mate's.

Her gaze dropped to the carpet in front of the fireplace. Suddenly, an overwhelming anger filled her with a rage she didn't think she was capable of feeling.

Although she knew Archer hadn't realized her father was listening, she figured he'd probably have said what he did no matter who was in the room. He'd been so livid, he'd struck out at the nearest thing—and that was her.

She could never trust a man who reached out to purposely hurt her.

But she could love him to the end of the earth.

More tears began flowing, slowly at first until finally, the sobs came from deep inside. Her voice echoed off the walls, sounding like the soft wails of a wounded animal.

Her tears continued to flow all afternoon. When they finally subsided, her eyes drifted closed and she slept on the very slice of carpet where she'd made such beautiful love to the man she'd just lost.

FOR THE NEXT three days, Archer immersed himself in work. He couldn't sleep more than a couple of hours at a time without being awakened by dreams. At that time he'd get up and work some more.

Thank God he had a catalog to get out, he told himself. He moved to the right and began snapping shots of the beautiful brunette posed on a muslin-draped, four-poster bed piled high with cream-and-white Battenburg pillows. "Keep moving, honey, you're beautiful," he said, finishing up the roll. When he'd shot the last frame, he stood and stretched. "That's it. You've done great, angel."

A makeup woman was on the spot, ready to freshen the model's blush and ensure there was no sheen under the hot lights. Archer rubbed the small of his back. He felt a hundred years old, today.

He forced a smile in the direction of the crew. "Okay, we're taking a break. Back here in fifteen minutes for the new set," he said, walking toward the darkroom. "Tracy, please arrange the set for the next shoot," he instructed his assistant.

"Will do," the young man answered.

Archer walked off. He needed to develop the film as soon as possible and get a contact sheet over to the catalog headquarters so they could make their choices.

But when he went into the darkroom, he shut the door and leaned against it with his eyes closed. It had been three long days since he'd gone to Melody's home and accused her of everything except crimes against the state. He'd felt so betrayed when his assistant had brought in the magazine and pointed out the article to him. In one minute, all his love for Melody went up in smoke. Anger had propelled him out his door and over to her apartment.

But as soon as he left her and stepped outside

onto the sidewalk, he knew he'd made the biggest mistake of his life.

He'd blamed the wrong person for all the right reasons. Then he compounded it by insulting her. And in case that wasn't enough, he'd insulted her family, too.

Then he'd gone home and tried to reach Sondra. Every hour. Every day. Early this morning was the first time the witch had let down her guard enough to answer the phone at work. Once he heard her voice, he hung up and went directly to her office and confronted her.

"It's all true! My sources are reliable, Archer!" she'd practically screamed. But he saw the lie in her eyes.

"You wrote that article just to hurt me. You played the vindictive woman scorned," he said, only then realizing just how spiteful she was capable of being. "You didn't give a damn about me. All you cared about was the prestige of being with me in public. Being seen. I was transportation to where you wanted to get."

"I loved you, Archer. But you didn't love me." It sounded like a whine. Hell, it *was* a lie—he could see it in her eyes. But she didn't want to admit it.

"You mean I didn't worship you and your ego?" he said disgustedly. "You want more than any man could ever deliver. It's a shame I didn't notice earlier. I guess you always did."

"You're a heartless man, Archer. Mean and cruel. I'm the one who told you about that auction to begin with," she said, her anger showing in her narrowed gaze. "But instead of thanking me, you gave your story to someone else. Unfair, Archer. I deserved that story."

Bingo. It all fell into place. The story was the problem, not Archer. She was talking about Shirley and Duane. He hadn't seen the official interview yet, but had heard it was being published in installments in the newspaper, along with the stories of several other auction guests. Sondra didn't know the publicity crew went with them, compliments of the charity. She just assumed he'd set it up.

"Jumping to conclusions again?" he questioned softly.

Her eyes turned to slits. "Whatever you're thinking, you're wrong. I was in love with you, Archer."

"But love is fleeting, isn't it? It's gone already. Now you're ready to hang me from the nearest flagpole."

Her chin lifted. "If you don't care, neither do I."

"Congratulations." He smiled without warmth. "If that's your criteria, then you never cared and this was done for spite."

Before she could answer, he walked out.

He felt victorious until he made it to the street. Then, thoughts of Sondra left his head and all the stuff he'd accused Melody of came crashing back down to weigh on his chest. He'd acted and spoken before he thought.

"Damn," Archer muttered aloud. With slow

precision, he began the process of developing the film.

He'd called Melody at least ten times, but had hung up immediately. He didn't know what to say. How the hell was he going to apologize for saying what he did right in front of her parents? They had almost as much right to hate him as she did.

Suddenly, he knew what excuse he could use to approach her. He reached for the phone on the wall and quickly dialed her number.

"Hello?"

The sound of her voice sent shivers down his spine and almost took his breath away. The ever-present ache expanded to fill his chest. "Melody, this is Archer," he said and thought he heard a small gasp. "Don't hang up. Please."

The line remained silent.

"I was reminded that we still haven't done the private publicity photo shoot. You paid for it, you know."

"The photo shoot?" She sounded unsure.

"Sure," he said, praying he sounded casual and easy. His stomach gave a lurch. "Remember? You were supposed to have publicity shots in this package."

Her tone hardened. "Thank you, but that won't be necessary," she said. Even now she was polite.

"No buts, Melody," he said firmly. "We need to set aside our differences and finish this for the charity's sake. Otherwise, the charity may not use this company again," he said, playing off her soft heart. "I've lost enough as it is."

"I see..." she said slowly. "Let me think about it."

"What's to think?" he pressed, scared to let go of the phone for fear he'd lose the thin connection with her forever. "Let's set it up now, and just go with it."

"Well, I..."

"Melody, Melody," he said, teasing her as if they were still together. As if he were still making love to her. As if he loved her. "Just say yes and we'll set a date and get it over with. Unless of course, you enjoy just blowing money for the..."

"Okay, okay. Yes, I'll do it. When?" She was irritated, but she was still talking to him. That was a good sign.

"How about next Friday?" he said quickly, not caring what was scheduled for then, he wasn't doing anything but be with Melody if he could talk long and fast enough to get her sweet little tush in here.

"What time?" she asked cautiously.

"Let's see," he said, pretending to look at his appointment calendar, which was outside at his assistant's desk. "I have four-thirty in the afternoon available."

"I have class starting at five-thirty."

Afraid of losing her, he shifted quickly. "Then how about ten in the morning?"

"I don't think this is a good idea."

"Don't quit now, Melody. You're almost finished with this project and me, for good. Do it right."

Apparently, he'd pushed all the right buttons. He knew because his heart was jump-started by her answer.

"Okay, ten o'clock Friday morning."

"Thanks," he said, trying not to let his relief come through the phone. "It'll be great."

"Well, okay, then," she said, her voice as hesitant as he felt her body to be that first time he kissed her.

"And Melody?" he said softly.

"Yes?"

"I apologize for what I said to you and your father. It never should have been said, and I certainly didn't mean to embarrass you."

"Please," she said in a choking voice.

God, he had a lot to pay for. The hurt in her voice hit him like a sledgehammer. His damn male pride. "I just wanted you to know."

"I know."

"Good, then I'll see you Friday. I'm writing it on my calendar so my assistant won't schedule anything all morning. That way we'll have an opportunity to shoot in Central Park, too."

"Archer, I wish…"

"I understand," he soothed. "I shot my mouth off too soon. It was just a glitch."

"No." Her voice was soft but definite. "It was much more than that."

In the studio, voices got louder as they came toward the darkroom and called his name.

He knew his time was up and yet was reluctant to let her go. "Look. We need to talk about this, Melody. I wasn't alone on this, but I'm apologizing for my part."

"It was all your part," she stated.

Someone banged on the door, calling his name. "Not all of it. Your father didn't help."

"Leave my family out of this, Archer. You intended to hang me up to dry by what you said. You just didn't realize how very wrong you were."

Banging continued. "Archer? Are you okay?" his assistant called.

"I've got to go, but we'll discuss this again," he promised. If he had anything to do with it, they were going to be together for a very long time, so they'd better resolve it now.

"No, we won't. If this is why you want to complete the project, then we can call it quits now."

"Melody,"

"No. We either get this done in laser fashion and no talk, or I'll cancel out now."

A shoulder hit the door. Damn. They were trying to break down the door!

"Just a minute!" he shouted. "We'll do the shoot," he said, giving in for the moment. "Talk to you Friday."

Before she could say no, he hung up.

"Just a minute!" he shouted, wanting to be left alone to gather his thoughts together. "I'll be right there!"

His heart beat heavily against his ribs. His breath was short and his desire to be with Melody was so strong he didn't know how he was going to make it through the shoot, let alone the rest of the week.

No wonder he'd never fallen in love before. Love was hell.

10

MELODY PRAYED HER SHAKING knees would hold through the ordeal. She'd gotten used to relationships going sour, but this time she was too in love to lose so easily. She had to confront her mother. It was time to lead her life with her own set of rules and regulations. And she had to make it plain to her parents—starting now.

She was meeting her mother for lunch in her favorite Italian restaurant. They would finally talk, and Melody knew her mother understood this because she chose a public place. Her mother was ensuring that Melody wouldn't shout or cry. After all, the Chase family name and training guaranteed that public displays would be frowned upon. No one knew when public episodes would be reported to the press or, worse, the tabloids. Just like that piece about her and Archer…she refused to think of it. She hurt enough already.

Walking into the restaurant took all her acting ability. Melody wore a smile that could fool most anyone. At least it worked on the maître d'. He gave an appreciative smile in return.

Her mother sat next to an interior window overlooking a garden with a small stone fountain that gurgled away, drowning sharp sounds. Smart move.

"Hello, Mother," she said, placing a light kiss on her mother's cheek. The older woman was dressed impeccably, as usual, wearing a brown silk suit with a matching brown blouse. Melody, too, wore a suit—one her mother had sent her for her birthday, along with another hundred shares of stock from her father's company. At least she looked the part of an adult female, even though she felt as raw as a hurt child.

"Hello, dear." Mrs. Chase's sharp gaze took in the forest-green plaid pantsuit and sand gold crepe blouse. She must have given it a good grade, because she smiled. "I hope this seating is good for you."

Melody sat down and gave a quick smile, more to reassure herself that this was the right step to take than to soothe her mother. "This is fine."

After staring at the menu for a moment, her mother ordered her normal meal; salad and bottled water with a twist of lemon. Melody decided to splurge, ordering pesto with foccacia bread and iced tea. The condemned man....

Her mother chose the conversation. "Your father and I have discussed our last breakfast with you." There was that regulation disapproving look. "Really, Melody. It's bad enough you read those books, but to attend an auction and bid thousands on a man like that Archer..."

"Are you against the money spent for literacy or the fact that I read those books?" She hesitated a moment before getting to the real thing. "Or is it the fact that Archer confronted Dad?"

"Honestly, Melody. You always had such an unusual way of looking at things."

That surprised her. "Really? I don't think of myself that way." Where in the world had her mother gotten such an idea?

Her mother's voice was quiet, barely above the sound of the rushing water. "You paid thousands, well that's all right. It's one of my favorite charities. Your father and I always support literacy." She sipped her water and Melody waited, knowing there was more. "But romance books. I haven't read any, but just from what I've seen on the covers, well. Melody, that's not real life."

Melody took a deep breath and promised herself she would not lose her temper. This was a discussion, not something to cause a scene about. She repeated that three times before she spoke. Quietly.

"I read those books because I enjoy stories that deal with strong women finding a relationship they can work with and through. I don't see anything wrong with that."

Her mother wasn't about to let any points get lost in the scoring. "But it fills your head with all kinds of dreams that aren't based on reality."

"You read mysteries and techno-thrillers, Mother. Does anyone accuse you of attempting to murder Dad? Or trying to blow up the world?"

Her mother looked shocked at the thought. "Of course not. Don't be silly."

Melody forced a smile on her lips. "I won't if you won't."

"Well," her mother said, obviously collecting her thoughts again and stalling for time. She wasn't used to having her daughter argue with her. Normally, if Melody disagreed, she remained silent. The rules were obviously changing.

Suddenly, for the first time in a long time, she felt equal to the task of discussion with her mother. Perhaps, even her father. All her life, she'd had opinions that she was afraid to mention in case she'd look silly or be wrong. But no more. It didn't matter how she looked. Archer had taught her that. She had to ask in order to learn. She had to learn to grow. She had to grow to stop the feelings of being inadequate.

The word finally came. It was *grown-up*. Right now, even while talking to her mother, she felt like a grown-up.

Her grin widened. She'd made it. She'd finally made it.

"Anyway," her mother was saying, "your father and I have been talking about what we could do to help you."

"Help me how? Enjoy your type of reading material? Make more money?"

"Find a husband, silly," Her mother said with a smile that meant she forgave her daughter for her earlier transgression. "Someone who loves you and will take care of you the way a woman should be taken care of. Someone who will be a good father and provider."

Good grief, she felt as if she were taking part in an old fifties movie. "Can't I take care of myself?"

"Your father has seen to the financial part, dear, but someone needs to handle the other parts."

"Mother, I'm a college professor. I would probably be a college professor even if Dad wasn't, well, Dad. That gives me a certain amount of capability. What parts can't I handle? Parts of what?"

Her mother looked irritated. "Don't bait me, Melody."

The waitress delivered the rest of their meal and set it before them. And Mrs. Chase, ever the lady, was agitated enough to speak while the waitress was still churning pepper. "There's nothing wrong with your father, Melody, and I resent your implying that he's some kind of monster. He's not. He loves both of us and does the very best he can to support us in our own needs."

"Our physical needs. Not our emotional ones," she said softly. "He's not involved in my life, Mom. He never was."

Her mother leaned forward. "Take care of your own emotional needs, Melody. That way you won't be hurt every time you turn around."

This was more enlightening than even her mother knew. She was finally understanding what their marriage must be like, and how empty it was for her mother. She felt sorry for her, but she wasn't willing to follow in her footsteps. "No, ma'am. I want more. I want to feel hurt. I want to feel happy. I want to have all the joys and heartbreak of an intimate, intertwined relationship."

"It doesn't sound healthy to me."

"Do you think I'm blind?" Melody made no pretense of her parents' relationship being what she wanted. "I can see what the loss of that emotional support has done to you two. It's like you're both isolated in the same house. You could be two ice cubes in the same fridge. That's not good enough for me. It's not fulfilling. I want more. Better."

"That's hurtful, Melody Chase."

She felt guilty but wasn't willing to back down. It was her turn to voice her own thoughts. "Mom, look, I love you and Dad lots. You know that. But I was raised watching you cater to him in a way that just plain makes me angry. It's as if you have no life other than to serve him."

"He's my husband," she stated stiffly.

"So who made him lord and master?"

"Melody," her mother stated the word as a threat.

But she wasn't ready to let the issue go yet. "Mother, you do what you do in your relationship with Dad in your own way. That's exactly what I *don't* want in my relationship with the man I love." What was that British expression? In for a penny, in for a pound? Well, this wasn't about money, it was about a relationship, which was just as precious. She took a deep breath and plunged in. "I need a different relationship. I need a man who respects me and wants to place our marriage above anything else he wants to do. I want a man who is willing to work as hard at being a husband as he works at his career."

"But darling," her mother said patiently, squeezing her hand, "that's simply not realistic."

"Then, if I can't have what I want and find someone who shares that viewpoint, I'll be happy to stay single for the rest of my life. I won't settle for mediocrity."

The older woman looked stricken. "No."

Melody gave it one more try. "Mom. You came into your marriage with a set of rules you both agreed to. I want the same option."

"Not with that young man with the shaggy hair and accusing eyes?"

Leave it to her mother to call a designer haircut shaggy because it wasn't the near crew cut her father wore.

"I love him." Tears stung her eyes. "But he doesn't love me enough to trust me. He needs to make it up the ladder of success on his own."

It was the tears that made her mother react. The older woman reached over and touched her daughter's hand. "I'm so sorry. What can I do to make it better?"

Melody had to smile. There was part of the problem. "Nothing, Mom. I have to work this out by myself."

"Then I won't be a grandmother any time soon," the older woman stated sadly.

"Not any time soon," Melody confessed.

Her mother leaned forward and reached for her hand once more. "Darling, you do realize that we love you very much, don't you?"

"Of course." And she did. Her parents might be chilly at times, but they tried hard to connect. She did appreciate that. Right now, with her newfound understanding, more than ever. She just wanted something different for herself.

She'd heard this before, but somehow, loving Archer made what her mother had said even more profound.

It was time to stop explaining what she wanted in a relationship and start finding a relationship she could work with. Everything else was hypothetical.

THREE DAYS LATER, with butterflies attacking her stomach, Melody packed a taxi with a garment bag full of the wardrobe changes Archer's assistant had told her to coordinate for the shoot. She didn't know how the photographic session was going to work out, but she knew she couldn't wait to see him just one more time. And some time during this shoot, she would tell him she loved him and wanted to be with him. If he still felt as if he'd been cheated, then at least she'd tried.

By the time she got to his apartment, the butterflies had invaded her entire body. She couldn't quell her excitement at seeing Archer again, despite the circumstances. Every night she'd gone to bed and dreamed of him. And she'd walked through every day doing things by habit because her mind was consumed with the man.

She loved him and this was an opportunity to see him again. She wasn't crazy, she was just anxious.

She was over half an hour early, but it didn't matter. She was here. His assistant could let her sit in a corner and wait until he was ready.

But when she knocked on the studio door and there was no answer, she became stubborn. She was Melody Chase, the woman who had already paid too much for this photo shoot to be left waiting around for someone else to take charge. Archer had asked her to do this, not the other way around. She wasn't going to stand in the hallway for half an hour.

Instead, she walked to his private apartment door and gave a solid knock.

She would not be ignored.

She knocked again.

When the door finally opened, her hand was raised to knock for a third time.

Instead, she stared.

A young woman with anger stiffening every part of her slim body stood just inside the door. She was dressed in a suit that looked as if it had seen better days. Her hair was swept back with a clip and the ends topped her head. But her narrow brown eyes were as stinging cold as chips of ice in a snowstorm.

"Well, if it isn't the next shift," she spat.

Melody's gaze flew past the woman to the

middle of Archer's large living area. Hands on his hips, he stood in the center of the room, handsomely naked except for a pair of black, form-fitting underwear.

Her arm lowered slowly and she fought to keep it by her side so she wouldn't tear into the woman's hairdo—while on her way to creating an artistic pattern of red scratches down Archer's broad shoulders.

She sucked in her stomach and held her breath. She would never allow the other woman to know how much this hurt.

She gave a half smile and arched a brow. "You really ought to put swinging doors here, Archer. It'd be so much easier on everyone."

"I don't need any damn door when the security guard will let anyone in uninvited this early in the morning." He dropped his hands from his hips and looked at the other woman in disgust. "If I had to guess, I'd say Sondra is willing to give whatever it takes to get the job done."

"And you're a job, all right," the woman stated with a harsh laugh. "And, by the way, if I wasn't right about the article, what's she doing here, darling? According to what I researched about this one, slumming wasn't part of her wardrobe before you. It must be that Archer...charm, again."

"Close your filthy mouth, Sondra. You don't know what you're talking about." Archer's voice was flat.

But Sondra wasn't about to disappear into the

woodwork. "I know enough," she stated angrily. "I know you used her as a substitute for me."

Archer ignored her. His gaze pinned Melody to the floor, both begging and denying the claim. "Melody. Don't believe this."

She put a hand on her stomach. Those butterflies had turned into battering rams. "I'm going to throw up. May I use your lap?"

He heard and never hesitated. "Yes."

"How touching," Sondra said sarcastically. "But then he always wallowed in slop, so what's the difference?"

"Shut up, Sondra. You're on your way out of here. You weren't invited, remember? This isn't the neighborhood pigsty."

Melody's chin came up. She would not make a scene or beg or cry. She would go through this with class. Her excellent upbringing came to the forefront. Years from now, when Archer was on his deathbed, he'd still remember her as one classy woman who had the willpower to remain strong to the end.

"We still have a shoot to do today," Melody said calmly. "I'll wait for you to get dressed, Archer. Say goodbye to your girlfriend here and then meet me in the studio." Melody bent down and picked up the garment bag, then walked through the interior door to the workroom that doubled as a hallway between his studio and private quarters.

"Melody, wait!" Archer called, but she didn't.

Tears pressed at her eyes and she wasn't about to let him see how much this scene had affected her. Instead she closed the doors behind her and then stopped.

She kept her hand on the light switch, but didn't flick it immediately. The voices from the other room rose, each calling the other names and adding hers here and there. Melody needed to catch her breath. To gather her forces and find the strength to continue this farce long enough to save face and walk away with her head held high and heart intact.

When she opened her eyes and flicked the switch, she was stunned.

One workroom wall held a row of filing cabinets, another a long table where negatives were scanned and sorted to be filed. Another held low cabinets where supplies and props were kept. All in all, the workroom was ordinary.

The walls, however, were not.

Sitting on the tables, strewn on the file cabinets, pasted to the walls and framed in snap frames of all sizes, shapes and colors, were photos—photos of Melody in the Poconos.

She was smiling, frowning, laughing, teasing, thoughtful, puzzled. Every emotion was documented in black and white and living color, from wallet-size all the way to poster-size.

She continued to stare, oblivious to the shouting going on in Archer's apartment. She paid no attention as she walked slowly around the room, stopping at each group of photos and staring. She hadn't realized how many he'd taken. Memories of each photo flooded her, bringing on the tears she'd fought so long and so well. Until now.

His caring, his talent, his way of speaking what was in his heart were all in those shots. But most of all, his love showed through. Especially in the pictures from their last day, when they'd spent time together without anyone else intruding.

He loved her.

He loved her!

He was so hurt about that article because he loved her. Just as she had felt so betrayed by his accusations because she loved him.

Love made all the hurt hurt more, but it also made all the wondrous feelings of laughter and joy and sorrow even more intense. It made her aware of caring, loving, of just plain being.

Melody stood straighter.

And if that little witch in the next room had her way, she would make sure that Melody never had the happiness she craved with the man she loved and wanted to be with.

Melody dropped her suitcases and placed her purse on top of them. Then, with unbelievable determination to pursue the life that she'd always sought, with the one man she wanted, Melody opened the doors and marched back into Archer's living room.

Grown-up time again.

Time to stand and fight instead of walking away. Time she acted like an adult woman instead of a young child rebelling against her parents. Time to go after what she wanted. And what she wanted was Archer.

Archer was standing in the bedroom door

opening trying to step into jeans, hopping around on one foot while informing Sondra in no uncertain terms where she should go.

Sondra was shouting in his face, calling him every name in the book while alternately promising to be exactly the kind of wife he wanted.

Melody's smile was grim. Fat chance.

She stood quietly by the workroom door for a moment before interrupting. "Sondra?" she said sweetly.

Sondra continued her tirade, but Archer had watched Melody enter the room. His gaze narrowed as he stood straight and zipped up his faded work jeans. His chest and feet were still bare. He certainly looked worth fighting for....

"Sondra?" Melody said again.

This time Sondra quieted enough to hear. She turned, her haughty stare strong enough to put anyone on the defense. Anyone but Melody. "You want something?"

"Yes." Melody smiled, but it never reached her eyes. "I want you to leave now. And Archer and I don't want to hear from you until you have permission to write up our wedding. Nicely."

"Dream on."

"I will. But you won't be around to see it." Melody opened the front door. "And by the way, thank you so much for enticing Archer to participate in the auction. He was by far the best bachelor there. And he certainly captured *my* heart."

"You're not really marrying him." Sondra gave a derisive laugh. "He's not the marrying kind."

"I am now," Archer said in a voice just as soft as Melody's. His velvet brown eyes devoured her and she felt the meaning of that gaze deep down inside her. It warmed her heart and boosted her confidence.

"See?" Melody said with a smile. "Archer is through with other women, and I thank you for this argument, Sondra. If I hadn't heard it, I might not have believed him when he asked me to marry him. But now I know he's telling the truth. He loves me enough to marry and have children."

Sondra's brows rose in disbelief. She looked back and forth at the two of them, her expression incredulous. "Archer? Children? The Archer I know wouldn't step foot in an arrangement like that. Don't you think you might have the wrong guy?"

Archer captured her gaze. Her eyes widened as she absorbed all the soft, personal messages he sent. Heat sizzled down her spine to rest in the pit of her stomach like warm, thick taffy. He took her breath away. Still.

"She's got the *only* guy," he said, his voice soft, but filled with determination. "For her, anyway."

Melody smiled slowly, her smile as intimate as his. She was so loved by this man, the same man she loved with all her heart.

As soon as Sondra disappeared, there would only be the two of them in the whole, wide world. And she wanted it that way....

"Oh," she said slowly, still looking at Archer.

"I've got the right guy, all right. No doubt about it."

"You're living in a dream world," Sondra exclaimed disgustedly. "But I'll let you find that out for yourself. Archer is selfish, always wants his own way. And you're too naive to know it."

Melody continued to stay connected to Archer by gazing into his eyes. She didn't want this moment to end and real life to intrude. Not yet...

"Thanks for your advice, but I'll follow my own path," Melody said firmly. "The door is open, Sondra whoever-you-are. Have a nice life."

Archer's small smile widened. "And please close it on your way out."

Silence was their answer. Then the door slammed shut with a loud crack that echoed through the large room.

Archer never let go of her gaze. Slowly, he walked toward her, reached out and wrapped his arms around her waist. He dragged her as close to him as clothing would allow, making sure she realized just how much he wanted her in his arms.

"Thank you," he said softly.

She looked up in surprise. "For what?"

"For fighting for me."

Her eyes lit up in delight. "I did, didn't I?"

"Yes. And I loved every minute of it."

She ran her hand over his still-bare chest. "You would. Two women fighting over a man has a tendency to feed the ego. Especially one as big as yours."

His grin deepened. "Of course. But when one of those women is the woman he loves, this man feels loved in return."

For just a moment, Melody's heart stopped beating. When it began again, it felt like a sledge-hammer against her ribs. "Don't tease me, Archer. It's not nice. Either say it again a thousand times or let me go."

"I love you, Melody Chase. I love you so much it damn—*darn* well hurts to even think of you not being by my side for the rest of our lives."

"Forever?" she whispered, loving every word he spoke.

He smiled, touching the side of her cheek. "You're in my head. I see you there, feel you, smell you. I love you so much, I don't think for-ever is enough time."

His mouth claimed hers as if she were a trea-sure. Her arms circled his neck and she clung to him as he kissed her.

When he pulled away, she rested her head on his chest and smiled. She'd never felt so happy, so complete....

She looked up. "And children? What do you think of children?" she asked, holding her breath.

"I think that both parents should be married— to each other—and that they should share in the child-raising responsibilities." He skimmed one hand up her side to cup a full, firm breast. "Mmm."

"And marriage? Are you talking marriage?"

she asked, her mind barely able to cope with the questions, let alone the answers.

"Marriage is good," he said as if thinking it over. "But only if we're talking about you marrying me."

"We're only talking about you and me," she repeated, changing the wording slightly.

His brows raised. "Are you proposing?"

Melody started to say no, then halted. It was time to keep the lead for a while. Bouncing Sondra out on her little fanny still felt good. Action felt good. "Yes." She paused. "Will you marry me, Archer?"

"Thank goodness this isn't sudden, or I'd have to be sweet and demure and give us time to get to know each other."

She didn't take the bait. Instead, she watched him silently, waiting for the answer she was now sure would come.

"But, since we do know each other, and since we do love each other, and since we are going to have a dozen children together, I guess I should say yes now and get it over with."

"Since I'd walk out of here if you didn't, I think you should say yes, too."

"Yes. Yes, I accept your proposal of marriage. Yes, I accept the fact that you desire my body. Yes, I accept that you want my mind. And I accept the fact that you admire my business acumen."

Despite knowing what he was going to say, she smiled. "Then you believe that I had nothing to do with that article."

"Of course. I knew it at the time."

"And you attacked me anyway?"

His eyes lost their mirth, becoming solemn. "No. I attacked you because you didn't tell me about your family. You let me read about who you were in some trashy magazine instead. And that article put the worst slant on everything I thought we'd meant to one another, making sure it hit every one of my buttons. It hurt, Melody. It hurt bad."

"But you knew who wrote it."

"Yes, but the information was still accurate. Sondra might have slanted the article, but she didn't outright lie."

"You believed her." It wasn't a question. It was a demand.

"I had wondered myself. Your apartment, your furniture and your clothing all pointed to more money than the usual university professor makes."

"But you never asked."

"I think I knew something was different, but I didn't want to know. Not yet."

"You'd rather get angry at the article."

"I was hurt. I loved you, I just didn't know how to express it yet."

She placed her head against his bare chest, hearing his heartbeat thudding heavily away. "When were you going to tell me you were hurt instead of trashing me in front of my parents?"

"As soon as you came over this morning for your photo shoot. And, if you recall, I didn't know your parents were there until it was too late." His arms tightened. "But, don't make the mistake of thinking I was letting you go again, Melody. You're mine and we're as good as married."

She chuckled. "Nothing is as good as married. We either are or we're not."

"That will change as soon as we get a license. If we—when we marry, will your parents try to interfere with my career?" That was definitely a question. She heard the doubt and knew it was his biggest worry.

"Hey," she said, slowly, holding his head in both her hands. "We're the married couple, remember? Our families comes *after* us."

"You're sure?"

She nodded. "I'm sure. I don't want my parents' marriage. I want ours. I want us to be involved, loving and as committed to each other as we are to what we do. I don't want to be an unseen appendage of you, Archer. I've seen too many marriages like that. I know it means more work, but I want us to enjoy life with each other, not pace the time away."

"Will I get to work at all?" he teased.

"Of course. I want to continue what I do while you continue on with what you do. But I want us working together on whatever else *we* do. Together."

"Together," he repeated, kissing the top of her head. He hesitated a moment. "And you still don't want to be a model?"

"And I still don't want to be a model." She

laughed. "My darling, I'll *never* want to be a model."

He nodded, finally reassured. But the smile in his eyes was working its way back into his sexy mouth. "I'm dreaming."

He let go of Melody with one arm and began walking slowly toward the bedroom. Her heart beat quickly in anticipation and she held on even tighter to his waist. "Where do you want to spend our honeymoon?"

"In bed," he said. "With a full moon shining above us."

"And a couple of good romance novels at the bedside."

"Honey, when we're through, you won't need romance novels."

They stopped by the side of Archer's bed. "Darlin'," she said. "I'll always need romance." She looked at him sternly. "And if you want to learn what a woman thinks, the best way to do it is to read what a woman reads."

"Yes, dear."

She grinned. "Thank you."

"Now, stop talking and get into bed and make love to your husband," Archer said.

"Not yet." She placed a hand on Archer's chest and asked the question she'd always wanted to know. "First, you have to tell me what my married name will be. After all, I may want to keep my own."

"Melody Archer."

"And I will call you…?"

"Darling."

He was truly exasperating. "And you will sign our marriage license as…?"

Archer leaned over and turned out the bedside light. Heavy curtains were drawn, letting in just enough light for her to see his firm body outlined against the windowed area.

"Yes."

"How?"

He gave a heavy sigh, then circled her waist and fell backward until they were both lying across the bed. Melody was on top, her fall cushioned by Archer's body. "Do you really have to know this?"

She kept her answer simple and direct. "Yes."

He gave a resigned sigh. "Rick."

"Rick Archer?"

"Yes."

She kissed his chin. "I love you, Rick Archer."

"You have to promise never to let anyone know."

"But why? It's a beautiful name." She rolled over and stared up at the ceiling fan. "Mrs. Rick Archer."

"Mrs. Archer. Period. I hate the name Rick. It sounds like a kid who plays the drums, not a grown, hardened man with a business of his own. Rick doesn't sound like a force to be reckoned with."

She dimpled. "Yes, darling."

Archer rolled over on her. "And just remember who's boss around here."

"Archer."

"No. Melody."

He kissed her then and stole her breath away. But that was okay with her. After all, he'd stolen her heart from the moment she'd seen him silhouetted in sunshine on the cabin porch.

It was time for that happily ever after she'd always dreamed about.

"Hey, big boy Ricky Archer," she stated huskily. "You wanna make babies?"

He never answered. But his actions spoke much louder than words....

TEMPTATION®

THE SEDUCTION OF SYDNEY by Jamie Denton

Blaze

Derek Buchanan's smitten with his gorgeous, leggy best friend Sydney Travers, and is planning to seduce her. So imagine his surprise when one night the beautiful brunette turns to him for comfort—and they have the most incredible sex! But how will Derek react when he finds out Sydney's expecting?

THE LITTLEST STOWAWAY by Gina Wilkins

Bachelors and Babies

Pilot and executive Steve Lockhart wanted to kick himself! He'd fallen head over heels for Casey Jansen, the woman of his dreams—*and* his business rival! It looked as if they would never get together—until he discovered an abandoned baby girl in his plane…

A CLASS ACT by Pamela Burford

Dena Devlin thought she'd be able to handle seeing old flame Gabe Moreau at their school reunion. After all, wasn't it thirteen years ago that Gabe had lost his innocence to someone else? But now she had a choice to make: reject her own desire and seek revenge…or get what she'd always wanted—Gabe.

WHO'S THE BOSS? by Jill Shalvis

Having inherited nothing from her father but a pile of bills and—horrors—an office job, Caitlin Taylor was suddenly a *poor* little rich girl. Worse still, she had the most infuriating, maddening and *gorgeous* boss, Joe Brownley. How long would it be until they realised business could be mixed with pleasure?

On sale 2nd June 2000

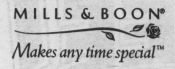

2 Books
and a surprise gift!

We would like to take this opportunity to thank you for reading this Mills & Boon® book by offering you the chance to take TWO more specially selected titles from the Temptation® series absolutely FREE! We're also making this offer to introduce you to the benefits of the Reader Service™ —

> ★ FREE home delivery
> ★ FREE gifts and competitions
> ★ FREE monthly Newsletter
> ★ Books available before they're in the shops
> ★ Exclusive Reader Service discounts

Accepting these FREE books and gift places you under no obligation to buy; you may cancel at any time, even after receiving your free shipment. Simply complete your details below and return the entire page to the address below. *You don't even need a stamp!*

YES! Please send me 2 free Temptation books and a surprise gift. I understand that unless you hear from me, I will receive 4 superb new titles every month for just £2.40 each, postage and packing free. I am under no obligation to purchase any books and may cancel my subscription at any time. The free books and gift will be mine to keep in any case.

T0EB

Ms/Mrs/Miss/Mr ....Initials................................
BLOCK CAPITALS PLEASE

Surname ....

Address ....

....

....Postcode ....

Send this whole page to:
UK: The Reader Service, FREEPOST CN81, Croydon, CR9 3WZ
EIRE: The Reader Service, PO Box 4546, Kilcock, County Kildare (stamp required)